RAVEN'S FEUD

From his sanctuary in Mexico, Raven heard of Beth Hallam's enquiries about him, so he travelled to Texas to stop her. After fruitless years hunting the outlaw Stig Ivey, he had sickened of that way of life. But now he was back and he had heard that Stig Ivey was coming. His prowess with a gun would be needed to face killers, rustlers, and the outlaws who had killed his kin. Raven knew his search for vengeance could not end until there was a bloody shoot-out.

CORBA SUNMAN

RAVEN'S FEUD

Complete and Unabridged

LINFORD
Leicester

First published in Great Britain in 2005 by
Robert Hale Limited
London

First Linford Edition
published 2006
by arrangement with
Robert Hale Limited
London

The moral right of the author
has been asserted

British Library CIP Data

Sunman, Corba
  Raven's feud.—Large print ed.—
Linford western library
1. Western stories
2. Large type books
I. Title
823.9'14 [F]

ISBN 1–84617–169–5

Published by
F. A. Thorpe (Publishing)
Anstey, Leicestershire

Set by Words & Graphics Ltd.
Anstey, Leicestershire
Printed and bound in Great Britain by
T. J. International Ltd., Padstow, Cornwall

This book is printed on acid-free paper

1

He had been in Mexico for his health, although he had never been ill. Tall and lean, travel-stained, he had ridden a far piece since dawn and now was well clear of the river they called the Big Muddy — that natural boundary between Mexico and Texas. The land was flat and barren, patched with scant grass — semi-desert. It was seemingly deserted, but he was keenly aware of his surroundings and moved cautiously towards the low hills that looked deceptively near but did not seem to draw nearer. His gaze was never still, shooting glances in every direction, looking for telltale signs that would betray an ambusher — birds rising suddenly from thick clumps of brush or animal wild life startled by some unseen human predator.

From time to time he halted the

black stallion and twisted in the saddle to study his backtrail. Once he snaked his Winchester carbine from its saddle holster and turned the horse around to cover the rough ground he had traversed, but there had been nothing to trigger him into action and he resumed his lonely trail, avoiding all likely ambush spots and staying off high ground.

He was called Raven — although his mother had christened him differently — a big man in a world of big men — four inches over six feet, powerfully built, wide-shouldered and narrow of waist. His body was honed to its physical peak by the style of life he had followed rigorously through ten years of riding the back trails of the great plains. Each year had added to the notoriety drawn to him by his doings. His angular face was passably attractive — dark eyes deepset, black hair that was thick at his nape and temples, a straight nose that sniffed the air for trouble like a dog, but his manner, bearing and appearance warned all and sundry that he was a man to be avoided.

Word had trickled south to the small Mexican town he had chosen for a refuge that a girl, Beth Hallam, in Dry Creek County, was asking about him, wanted him to go to her aid, and would pay handsomely for his time and trouble. He had ignored the whispers but her efforts had attracted the attention of others who were interested in his whereabouts and he had already killed a bounty hunter who made the mistake of trying to collect the price on his head that had been set for a killing which had been self-defence. He had finally received an impassioned letter from the girl, pleading for his help, and was riding north now to find her and put an end to the agitation she stirred up around him. He had taken a lot of trouble to lose himself in Mexico, for these days he would do anything for a quiet life, but the girl's attempts to locate him had rekindled unwanted interest in him, and if he did not stifle her efforts he could see himself being forced back into his old way of life.

His dark eyes glittered as he looked around, already recognizing landmarks that he had thought never to see again. The lines on his face deepened as he considered the risk he was taking. Word of his return north of the border would inevitably reach all those drifting gunhands whose desire for the reputation of being known as the man who had killed Raven would inevitably bring them to confront him. Over the years he had been forced to kill a number of their breed but had wearied of the slaughter. They had given him no peace, had been like flies buzzing around him, never to be ignored.

Flushed out of his retirement, he was determined to stop Beth Hallam's agitation before slipping back into Mexico to resume his peaceful life. Already he was aware of the sense of danger and loneliness that was returning to his mind. He had been like a hunted animal before seeking refuge in

Mexico, had needed months of relaxation before finding a sense of peace, but recrossing the border into harsh reality had already brought back to him all the cautions and worries that had attended his former life. Eight days had passed since he started north and now he was feeling like a wolf with the whole world pitched against him.

He smiled coldly as his thoughts drifted over his past. Such had been his desire to escape the eternal round of vigilance and violence surrounding him that he had turned his back upon the one great passion that had for years discoloured his life — the hunting down and killing of Stig Ivey and those gunmen who had been responsible for the deaths of his mother and younger brother ten years ago — innocent bystanders caught up in the Ivey gang's attempt to pull off a double bank robbery — shot down in the murderous crossfire that had beaten off the gang. Even that desire had been discarded in his search for peace, but now all the old dark emotions were rampant again in his calculating mind and he doubted if he could ever return to Mexico. The wolf had left its lair and the deadly Nemesis blighting his life had brought him again to the trail of no return.

His thoughts were eternal as he crossed the trackless wastes towards the raw civilization of Clayville, a sprawling town that, by its position, marked the jumping off spot for any and every destination in Texas. It was near there that Diamond Cross, the Hallam cattle ranch, was situated, and where he hoped to persuade Beth Hallam to stop her attempts to hire him.

The torturous sun, heading for the peaks of those distant mountains, swung slowly behind their lonely bulk to delineate them with red-gold fire, and long purple shadows were cast out across the range, bringing relief from the intolerable heat that had baked the world during the long hours of daylight.

Raven halted and dismounted stiffly as night came to cover his presence with dense shadows. He poured water into his hat from his canteen and used his neckerchief to moisten the muzzle of his black horse. The animal whickered softly in appreciation and Raven patted its dusty neck as he peered around into the impenetrable darkness and listened for unnatural sound. He remained immobile until stars brightened the deep gloom of the high-vaulted sky, and when the pale moon gained a brighter intensity and illuminated the range with soft light he mounted and continued, following no known trail as he relied upon his memory to get him to his destination.

It was well into the evening when he spotted a straggle of yellow lights in the distance, and a coldness settled in his chest as he regarded them. Clayville, he remembered, was nothing more than a stark collection of adobe buildings, and all his instincts warned against entering the place. Although it had been more than five years since his only visit, someone there was bound to recognize him, and word of his presence would flare like a prairie fire, with the resultant reaction from the local law that had sickened him of life on the dodge.

Raven dismounted on the outskirts of the town and tethered his horse in the brush. He entered the street slowly, senses hair-triggered. Shadows were dense. His dark eyes were narrowed and alert, probing his surroundings, and his right hand was close to the holstered pistol in his low-slung holster. His horse needed a rest and he was gaunt from the week-long ride from the south, but he had learned long ago never to take chances with his life so the comforts would have to wait. He was expecting a reception committee to be waiting for him with a surprise sixgun party in his honour, for Beth Hallam had not kept her motives secret, and he moved like a shadow towards the livery barn to check it out. His nerves were taut and he was ready to flow into instant and deadly action.

He passed a noisy saloon, stifling an

impulse to stop off for a much-needed drink, and stayed in dense shadow, watching for armed men. He reached the end of the sidewalk without incident, his eyes well accustomed to the night, and stood at the corner of a store, watching the stable. Minutes passed and nothing aroused his suspicion, but he was not satisfied. He smelled trouble, and remained watching, prepared to wait half the night. He could hear the muted sound of a piano being pounded in one of the saloons, the sharp tinkling notes being carried on a breeze coming from the north. The heat of the day was dissipating slowly. He felt uncomfortable, sweating, hungry, thirsty. He mentally cursed the unknown Beth Hallam for causing this situation.

Boots sounded on the sidewalk at his back, coming towards him, and Raven slid around the corner of the store and dropped his right hand to the butt of his deadly gun. The boots came nearer, and stopped at the corner less than a yard from where Raven was standing. He did not move, watching the indistinct figure, wondering if he had been spotted or not.

'You seen anything yet?' The newcomer moved slightly and Raven caught the glint of metal on the front of the man's shirt. A law star! He did not move. 'Well?' the man continued. 'I asked you if you've seen anything. I know I said for everyone to be quiet, but you can speak. Any sign of Raven yet?'

'No.' Raven did no more than breathe his whispered reply.

'Who are you?' The lawman spoke irritably. 'I didn't put anyone here. Where are you supposed to be waiting?'

Raven knew that in another second the lawman would realize that he was addressing a stranger. He set his feet and swung his right shoulder backwards slightly, then whirled in a pivot of shifting weight and smashed his right fist against the lawman's jaw. He reached out, grasped the man's powerful body as it floundered backwards, then lowered it to the sidewalk. There had been practically no sound but almost immediately a voice called from the shadows to Raven's left.

'Who's there? Is that you, Frank? What's all the noise about?'

Raven straightened and slid around the corner to move away. He had learned all he needed to know. A reception had been prepared for him and he would be a fool to stick around. He crossed the street and paused in the darkness to look back at the corner, and saw a man appear and bend over the motionless lawman. The next instant the man was yelling an alarm, and Raven entered an alley to his right and headed for the back lots.

A gun was fired somewhere at his back and he heard the echoes racketing back and forth across the street. The slug came nowhere near him and he smiled and kept moving, returning to his horse. He mounted and departed from the vicinity of the town, his hunger unappeased. Life on the dodge was a thankless existence.

As he rode he looked for a campsite, and halted when he found a small area of scrub grass that would enable the black to line its belly with something resembling food. He rummaged in a saddle-bag, found some jerky, and sat on his bedroll to eat it. Poor fare indeed! But this was how it was for a man riding the back trails. He stretched out and slept the rest of the night away, awakening just before dawn to survey his bleak surroundings with jaundiced eyes.

He was out of food and coffee, and breaking camp, turned back to Clayville and circled the town to approach from the north. The livery barn was the first building on the left, with its attendant corrals, and he dismounted at a water trough to stand looking around while the black took a long drink. He pulled the animal away before it had taken its fill, and led it into the barn, where a youth of about eighteen was cleaning out the stable.

'Howdy, mister.' The youth put down his pitchfork and came forward, smiling. 'I been left in charge here until Uncle Matt gets back. Looks like your hoss has travelled a far piece.'

'Take care of him.' Raven produced a dollar. 'He's had some water. Let him take his fill after he's eaten. Give him the best. He's earned it. When I come back, if he tells me you've done him proud, you can keep the change out of this dollar.'

'Gee, thanks. I'll treat him like I would my mother, sure as my name is Danny Delf. I sure hope he can talk when you get back.'

Raven grinned and departed. He walked along the street to a restaurant, and found it busy, but there was an empty table and he sat down heavily. The smell of bacon and beans stirred his appetite and he looked around while waiting for a busy waitress to get to him. He saw a big man with a law star on his vest sitting across the room, and the man was staring at him with an intentness that alerted Raven. The waitress stopped by the table at that moment and Raven ordered breakfast. By the time she went into the kitchen the lawman was on his feet and coming towards Raven's table.

'You're a stranger.' The deputy's tone was hard and belligerent, his ugly face not enhanced by his scowl. His dark eyes were cold, unfriendly, filled with suspicion. His right hand was resting on the butt of his holstered pistol. 'Who are you and what's your business around here?'

'I'm Pete Drake. I'm looking for a riding job. I'll be making a round of the local cattle spreads when I've eaten.'

'Where you from? Have you come up from across the border?'

'Nope. Never been to Mexico, and I don't hanker on going. Texas is as far south as I want to go. I've come down from Abilene, and reckon to stick around here for a spell, if I can get a riding job.'

'There's trouble brewing in these parts.' The lawman shook his head, still suspicious. 'You don't look like a wandering cowpoke. I reckon the only time you touch beef is when it's handed to you on a plate.'

'So what am I?' Raven's eyes bored into the deputy.

'You could be Raven, the gunslinger. He's due to show up around here, so I hear. We figured he was in town last night, when a man answering Raven's description hit Sheriff Wilson — broke his jaw with a single punch.'

'I've heard of Raven. Real fast with a gun. I'm sure glad not to be wearing his boots. But you don't really think I'm him.'

'What makes you say that?'

'You wouldn't brace me alone if you did. It would be sudden death to try and take Raven by yourself.'

'I guess you're right. I'm Clint Jackson, deputy sheriff.' His tone seemed to ease a couple of notches. 'So you're looking for a riding job, huh?

15

Drop by the law office when you've eaten and I'll show you a map of the county — point out some of the spreads you might try for work.'

'Thanks. That's a good idea.' Raven held Jackson's gaze. 'My poke is nigh empty. If I run outa dough you could arrest me for vagrancy.'

Jackson grinned and nodded. 'We're tough on vagrants around here.' He turned away. 'See you around.'

Raven watched the big man depart, and was not fooled by his sudden friendliness. It could be that Jackson had gone for some extra guns to back his play. He dropped his right hand to the butt of his .44 Smith & Wesson, let it rest there until the waitress returned with his meal, then began to eat with the eagerness of a near-starved man.

The restaurant was almost deserted by the time he finished his meal, and he left a tip for the waitress when he arose from the table to depart. She came to collect his plate as he stood up and he dropped back into the seat.

'I'm a stranger in town.' His face eased out of its customary hardness and he smiled. 'I've got to find myself a job pronto. I guess you know pretty much what is going on around the county. Are any of the cattle spreads taking on riders?'

The girl paused with his plate in her hand. She looked hot and harassed. Her brow was damp and her face had that washed-out look that came from over-working. She had blue eyes and fair hair, but seemed subdued by worries.

'There are a lot of gunnies in the county.' She pushed back a lock of straying hair that stuck damply to her forehead.

'You figure me for a gunnie?' Raven smiled. 'That's funny. So did the deputy. He thought I was Raven, the gunslinger.'

'Be careful around Jackson.' Her voice was low, intense. 'He's real dangerous. Get on the wrong side of him and you'll find nothing but trouble.

If you really want a riding job then you could do worse than try Rafter B. I do know Floyd Buxton is looking for extra riders who are handy with a gun.'

'Thanks. And you figure I fit the bill, huh? What is it about me that gives you that impression?'

'The way you wear your gun and the mannerisms that go with it. I had a brother who lived by his gun, and I remember only too well how he acted and reacted until he met someone who was faster. He's in the cemetery — been there eight years, and would still be under thirty if he had chosen a different profession.'

Raven nodded. 'Thanks for the information. If I wanted to go to Diamond Cross, how would I get there from town?'

'I heard tell that Beth Hallam is hoping to hire a top gun.' Her blue eyes lifted for a moment to look into his set face. 'Are you the man she's waiting for?' She paused, then said, 'Sorry. It's none of my business, I wouldn't want to know anything about you even if you felt like telling me. Diamond Cross is out there to the north-west. Just ride in that direction and you can't miss it. The Hallams own everything out that way, or think they do. If you want to ride for Diamond Cross then you could talk to the sheriff. He's real friendly with Lorne Hallam, Beth's father.'

'Thanks for the information.' Raven turned away and walked to the door.

He peered out through the window at the street before opening the door, looking for signs of trouble. The sidewalks seemed to be clear and he departed, pausing with his back to the door to survey the street. His right hand was down at his side and very still, ready to flash into action at the drop of a hat. He saw nothing to trigger him and went along the sidewalk, heading for the stable, having no intention of visiting the law office.

He felt uneasy, walking through the town in broad daylight, and there was a tingling sensation between his shoulder blades. He paused to look in the window of a gun shop, using its reflections to check his surroundings. The town seemed unusually quiet for the time of morning, but he saw nothing to arouse his suspicions and moved on to the end of the sidewalk where he halted on the spot where he had hit the sheriff the night before to gaze across the wide expanse of dust between him and the stable.

His instincts were working at full stretch and he was wary of going into the barn at this time. He had an itch in the palm of his right hand, a telltale warning of impending trouble, and flexed his long fingers. There had been a reception organized for his arrival, and he didn't think the sheriff would call off his men just because he had collected a broken jaw. He stepped off the sidewalk and his long stride rapidly covered the distance to the stable. If an ambush was awaiting him then he had no option but to spring the trap.

Raven reached the wide doorway of

the barn without incident and paused beside it to listen intently, looking along the length of the street for anything to raise an alarm in his mind. He grimaced. It was too quiet. He moved quickly then, stepping into the barn and easing to one side, his dark eyes sweeping the dim interior. His hand was on the butt of his gun. A horse stamped in one of the stalls and his pistol leapt into his hand. His eyes glinted coldly as he moved to his right. Where was Danny Delf?

He was about to move to locate his horse when several pieces of straw floated down from the loft. His gun muzzle lifted, covering the loft ladder and the shadowy space beyond.

'I got you covered,' he rasped, the sound of his voice echoing in the close stillness. 'Whoever you are, show yourself, then come down the ladder. You got five seconds before I start shooting.'

'Don't shoot. I'll come down.' There was an immediate rustling overhead and more straw floated down from the loft. A slim figure came into view and began to descend the ladder. 'I'm a friend of Danny Delf. He's gone for coffee. He told me there was a real live gunnie in town, and reckons you are Raven. I wanted to see you, so I hid up here.'

Raven covered the figure with his pistol as it descended, and was surprised, when it reached the ground and turned to face him, to find it was a girl in her teens, dressed in pale-blue pants and a blue denim jacket. Big blue eyes gazed at him with fear in their depths.

'I know all about you, if you are Raven,' she said breathlessly. 'I'm Sarah Jane Wisbee. My father owns the bank. Beth Hallam is my friend, and she's told me about you. Are you Raven? You fit the description Beth gave me.'

'So does a hundred other men.' Raven lowered his gun, uncocked and holstered it, but did not relax his vigilance. His ears were strained for suspicious noise inside and outside of the big barn. 'I reckon you're playing a mighty dangerous game, Miss Wisbee. Are you trying to get yourself shot?'

'No. I'm trying to save you from being shot. The law is hoping to get you through Beth's attempts to bring you on to her side in her trouble.'

'How's a female got such trouble she needs a gunnie to get her out?'

'Her father owns Diamond Cross. He was bush-whacked six months ago, crippled by a shot in the back. Beth runs the ranch and she's been up to her neck in trouble ever since. She hit on the idea of sending for Raven, him being the fastest gun there is. She heard he was in Mexico, and thought he would come to help her if she paid him enough.'

'And he hasn't turned up, huh? And everyone around here has been watching for Raven, ready to believe that any stranger who looks anything like him is the real thing. What's going on around here, anyway? Who's making trouble for

23

Diamond Cross?'

At that moment Raven caught the sound of a boot scraping the hard ground just outside the door. His eyes swivelled towards the wide doorway, and Sarah Jane Wisbee's eyes widened when she saw his pistol suddenly appear in his right hand, the movement a blur of amazing speed.

Raven grasped the girl's arm and pulled her away from the doorway, cautioning silence. He listened intently, and tensed when a harsh voice called raucously from outside. 'Raven, we know you're in there. You ain't got a chance. The place is surrounded by possemen, and they have orders to shoot to kill if you resist. Come on out with your hands up.'

'That's Clint Jackson, the deputy sheriff,' Sarah Jane said tensely. 'He's a bad man to cross. What are you going to do, Raven? Will you shoot the entire posse to get away?'

'I'm not gonna shoot anybody.' Raven replied. 'Just stay quiet and I'll talk my way out of this.'

'Not with Jackson running things. He's a man with no sense at all. If he thinks you're Raven then as far as he's concerned, that's who you are. Don't trust him an inch. He'll trick you if he can.'

Raven suppressed a sigh. He saw an armed man peer into the barn through the wide back door that gave access to a rear corral. The man ducked backwards quickly, then eased forward for another peek inside.

'Hold it, Jackson,' Raven called. 'I'm coming out.'

'Throw out your gun first,' the deputy replied. 'Don't try any tricks or you're dead.'

'You better not start any shooting,' Raven warned. 'I've got Sarah Jane Wisbee in here with me.'

'I'll go out first, if you like,' Sarah Jane said, and although there was fear in her eyes her chin was tilted resolutely.

'Don't you harm that gal,' Jackson

warned. 'Come on out so we can look at you. If you ain't Raven then you got nothing to worry about. But toss out your gun before you show.'

Raven uncocked his pistol and threw it out through the doorway. At that moment he held a very low opinion of the unknown Beth Hallam, for she had brought him to this. He held up a hand as Sarah Jane started forward to the doorway.

'Stay here,' he said curtly. 'I don't hide behind a woman's skirts.'

He turned and walked out of the barn and into the sunlight, raising his hands shoulder high as he did so.

2

Jackson was standing with his back to the front wall of the barn, a double-barrelled shotgun in his hands. There were two armed men with him, and one of them stepped forward to jab the muzzle of a Winchester against Raven's ribs. Jackson's mean features expressed pleasure and his narrowed eyes gleamed.

'I got you,' he exulted. 'Hands up. A gunnie like you carries more than one gun. Search him, Billy, and you watch him good, Mike. If he so much as blinks then you let him have it.'

'It looks like you don't believe me,' Raven said quietly. 'I told you I'm not the man you're looking for, so what have I got to do to prove I ain't Raven?'

'There's a man in the county who knows Raven by sight.' Jackson's coarse face was lined with brutal anticipation

27

as he picked up Raven's discarded gun. 'I'll get word to him to come into town and take a look at you. I'm gonna put you in the jug until he gets here.'

Raven tensed at the deputy's words but his face betrayed no emotion. 'I doubt you got anybody who can recognize me,' he replied. 'I'm a stranger in these parts. Never been this far south before.'

'We'll see about that.' Jackson moved into the doorway of the barn and peered around. 'Where you got to, Sarah Jane? Come on out of there and tell me what in hell you were doing with a killer like Raven.'

There was no reply, and at that moment Raven caught the sound of receding hoofs coming from the rear of the stable. Jackson heard also and ran through the barn to the back door.

'Sarah Jane, come on back, you hear?' Jackson shouted across the back lots. 'I wanta talk to you. Come back. You got some explaining to do, gal. I ain't letting you get away with anything after that last time you made a fool outa me.'

The departing hoofs continued until they died away.

Jackson came back to the front door, shaking his head and cursing softly. He confronted Raven, his weathered face set in ugly lines.

'What were you doing with that gal?' he demanded.

'Not a thing. She was saddling up when I came in for my horse.' Raven met the deputy's hard gaze, his face expressionless, his tone neutral, concealing his instinctive dislike of this big lawman.

'And where were you heading before I came along and stopped you?' Jackson grinned maliciously.

'Out to Diamond Cross. I told you I need a job.'

'Not now, you don't. You ain't going no place but jail.' Jackson shook his head. 'I got a nasty feeling about you so I reckon we better get on to the jail and see what the sheriff makes of you. I figure you're the man who hit him last night, and if you are then you better start worrying about your future. Come on. I'm gonna put you in a cell until I can find out more about you.'

Raven did not argue, and walked beside the deputy with the two possemen trailing them, covering him with their weapons. He was thinking up a few hard names for Beth Hallam, aware that he would still be in Mexico but for her attempts to locate him.

They had just entered the street when the sound of rapidly approaching horses sounded behind them. Jackson swung around and a curse spilled from him as he halted. Raven glanced over his shoulder and saw Sarah Jane Wisbee coming back into town, accompanied by a young woman and two tough-looking men.

'Jeez!' Jackson's pistol was in his right hand and he lifted it then lowered it again, keeping it at arm's length by his side. 'This ain't gonna be my day. Either one of them females on the prod is pure trouble, but the pair of them together is more than any one man can handle. Someone should keep them on a tight rein. They sure take the shine off my life when I set eyes on them.'

Raven studied the woman riding beside Sarah Jane and his interest quickened. She looked feminine despite wearing range clothes — close-fitting leather pants and a short leather jacket which did not conceal the curves of her slender body. Chestnut curls peeped from under the flat brim of her small Stetson. Her features were well-formed, attractive, and her brown eyes showed stormy determination in their dark depths as they studied Raven's big figure. It was plain to him that she liked what she saw. Her gaze was intent as she studied him, and he was reminded of a cougar gazing at its prey.

'What's going on here, Jackson?' She spoke sharply, her right hand lifting to the butt of a Smith & Wesson American .44 that was holstered at her waist. It was a fancy-looking pistol, silver-plated and scroll-engraved, with an ivory grip. There was an unspoken challenge in her attitude, and Jackson cursed under his breath.

'Say, I don't want no more trouble with you, Miz Hallam,' he said in a rush. 'This is law business and you better keep out of it.'

'Sarah Jane was hightailing it out of town to see me at Diamond Cross when I met her. She said you were rousting a stranger you figured to be Raven. Well, the man you got there ain't that lowdown killer.' Beth's gaze was fixed on Raven's face as she spoke, and although he recoiled mentally at her description of his way of life his face remained expressionless. 'I saw Raven once, about four years ago, and I can tell you that this man doesn't resemble him beyond being about the same build. Raven has a real killer's face. His eyes are like broken glass. He looks like he'd shoot his own mother if the chips were down. And do you think he'd let himself be taken by a second-rate deputy?'

Jackson flushed and looked down at his gun, clearly confused by the girl's scathing tone.

'I'm only doing my duty as I see it,' he said, and thrust his pistol deep into its holster, removing his hand from it as if the butt had suddenly become too hot to touch. He held Raven's gun in his right hand.

'Then it's a good job for you I came along when I did. You don't often get the chance of saving yourself from acting like a fool.'

The tart note in Beth's voice stung Jackson. His face took on a deep red flush and then showed ugliness. His lips tightened and he scowled.

'There ain't no need to talk to me like that,' he rasped. 'Are you sure this man ain't Raven? You said you saw Raven once. Where was that? What did he look like? What was he doing at that time?'

'Heading into Mexico, I think. He looked real mean, with the coldest eyes you ever saw. He stopped at Diamond Cross for food, and one of the crew who knew him by sight told me it was Raven. I sure was glad when he left the spread.'

'I'll take your word for it that he ain't Raven,' Jackson said firmly, 'but only if he goes to Diamond Cross and works there until I can run a check on him.'

Beth Hallam turned her full attention to Raven, her dark eyes alive with interest.

'Are you a range man, mister?'

'Sure thing, and right now I need a riding job.'

'What's your name and where do you come from?'

'I'm Pete Drake. I've worked my way south from Kansas, and reckon to stick around here for a spell.'

'I'll give you a job, but there's trouble on this range and if you come to Diamond Cross you would be expected to fight for the brand. Can you use a gun?'

'As well as the next man, I guess.'

Raven took his gun from Jackson and slid it into his holster. 'What kind of trouble you having?'

'Someone is out to take Diamond Cross from the Hallams and I mean to stop them.' She spoke firmly. 'Get your horse and ride out to the ranch with me. I can put you to work.'

'That wouldn't be a good idea, Beth,' one of her two tough-looking companions said harshly. 'Sheridan wouldn't like that.'

Raven turned his attention to the girl's companions. Both had the earmarks of gunhands, alert, hard-bitten, and a tremor passed through him as his nerves tightened. He did not want to get caught up in local events, but had to go along with the appearance of wanting a job while Jackson stood watching.

'Sheridan will have to do the other thing then,' Beth observed. 'Do you want to ride for me, Drake? If so, your first job is to shoo away these two saddle-bums. I don't like them riding with me. They've been sticking to me like a burr under my saddle, acting on the orders of Ham Sheridan, the Diamond Cross foreman. Send them back to the ranch.'

Raven nodded. He did not move, and merely said, 'You heard the lady. Make tracks outa here.'

One of the men began to wheel his mount but the other stood his ground.

'I got my orders from Sheridan and no Johnny-come-lately is gonna throw his weight around me,' he blustered.

'You got new orders now.' Raven smiled. 'Get the hell out.'

The Diamond Cross gunman reached for his pistol in a fast draw. His weapon was halfway out of its holster before Raven moved in a blur of speed, his gun appearing in his hand and exploding with a crashing roar. Gunsmoke plumed from the muzzle and the gunman's hat flew from his head. The man paused, holding his gun half-drawn, and stared into the muzzle of Raven's steady gun, shocked by the turn of events.

'The next slug will be between your eyes,' Raven said softly. 'Turn around and split the breeze or continue your draw. The choice is yours.'

The man thrust his pistol deep into its holster and turned his horse. He rode away without looking back, his back stiff, his hands well clear of his waist. The second rider gazed at Raven for a moment, then turned and followed quickly. Raven felt a thread of despair unwind in his breast as he realized that he was being hooked against his will.

'Very good.' Beth Hallam smiled. 'What did you think, Jackson? Aren't you glad I came along when I did? It looks like I saved you from a lot of grief.'

'It ain't none of my business.' The deputy's face was set in harsh lines. 'I'm only interested in the law. I'll be out to Diamond Cross to see you, Drake, when I get some real evidence.'

'You come to Diamond Cross and I'll

set the dogs on you,' Beth countered. 'I'm trying to clean up my range. Get your horse and ride with me, Pete, and keep your hand on your gun. I need to visit the store before riding back to the ranch. You'll find me there.'

She touched spurs to her brown mare and entered the town at a canter, sided by Sarah Jane. Raven glanced at the two discomfited Diamond Cross riders moving steadily to the north-east, then looked at Jackson. The deputy was gazing after Beth Hallam, an ugly expression on his coarse face.

'One of these days that gal is gonna get her come-uppance.' Jackson glowered, hatred showing in his face. 'It ain't right that she rides around the range throwing out orders like she's the boss. Say, you don't know what you're getting into, Drake. If you did you'd rather stick your hand in a nest of sidewinders than take a job with Diamond Cross and ride out with that gal. She's hell on wheels, and then some. Hell, if I don't feel sorry for you!

It would be better if you let me lock you in the jail than go up against the men you will have to face.'

'Thanks for the advice.' Raven turned and went into the stable for his horse, and when he rode out a few moments later the deputy and his two possemen had gone. He cantered into town, making for the store, and was prepared to tell Beth Hallam that he had no intention of working for her. In ten minutes he could be clear of town and heading back to Mexico without a care in the world.

A buckboard was being loaded with supplies in front of the general store, and Raven tethered his horse beside the brown mare Beth Hallam had ridden into town. He dismounted and stood beside the black, waiting for the girl to emerge from the store, and when she did not appear after some minutes he stepped up on to the sidewalk and lounged in the shade of the awning, watching the street and his surroundings, his right hand never far from the flared butt of his deadly pistol.

Five minutes passed and Raven grew impatient. He had spotted Sarah Jane's horse standing in front of the bank and assumed that the two females had separated. He moved to the doorway of the store and peered inside. A tall, thin man wearing an off-white apron was coming to the door, toting a large box. He subjected Raven to a keen glance, and Raven stepped aside for him, then entered the store while the man went out to the buckboard.

There was no sign of Beth Hallam in the store, and Raven frowned as he looked around. An oldish woman was serving behind the counter, chatting to a middle-aged female customer. Raven faced the store-keeper, who was returning through the doorway.

'Beth Hallam was in here,' Raven said.

'She ain't now,' came the surly reply. 'I told her I can't fill her order no more and she left.'

'You refused to serve her?' Raven was

surprised. 'Why would you turn away good custom?'

'What's it to you? Ain't you the stranger Clint Jackson was gonna arrest?'

'I asked you a question, mister, and I expect an answer.'

The storeman looked intently into Raven's dark eyes and read something there that amended his attitude.

'I get my orders around here like most everyone else,' he said, 'and I do like I'm told or get a hatful of trouble. I was told to bar Beth Hallam from the store and that's what I did. If you don't like it, mister, then go talk to the man who gives the orders. It ain't got nothing to do with me, sure as my name is Jake Meagher. Go rattle the bars of Monte Grand's cage and see for yourself what kind of a wildcat he is. Me, I got honest work to do.'

'Who's Monte Grand?'

'The big augur around here. What he says goes — or else. He owns everything in town, except my store and

41

the livery barn, and he runs a tough crew out at Big G to keep folks in line.'

'Where will I find Grand?'

A glint appeared in Meagher's eyes as he grinned. 'His office is next to Lappard's Saloon, but these days he's mostly out at his ranch. He's got tough men managing his affairs, and Homer Kirk is the man you need to see. He'll be in his office now. After you've seen him, come back and let me know how you got on.'

Raven departed, and stood for a moment on the sidewalk, looking at Beth Hallam's mare. He was frowning as he swung into his saddle and rode along the dusty street, passing Lappard's Saloon and the Monte Grand office beside it, which he subjected to a keen scrutiny. He did not stop until he reined in beside Sarah Jane's horse standing at the hitching rail in front of the bank.

The bank door opened as he approached it and Sarah Jane emerged, looking as if she had received harsh treatment at someone's hands. The girl stopped in mid-stride at the sight of him, and then came forward to grasp his arm.

'Don't go in there,' she said firmly. 'My father is not in a good mood this morning.'

'I don't care about your father. I'm looking for Beth. She seems to have disappeared.' Raven explained the situation and saw the girl's face become distressed.

'It's your fault,' she accused. 'You chased off the two men guarding her. Why do you think they were with her?'

'Hold your horses. I only did what she told me. Are you telling me it ain't safe for her to show up alone in town?'

'She's disappeared, hasn't she?'

'I figured she'd come to you here.'

'Leaving her horse at the store? Beth never walked a step if she could ride. Something bad has happened to her.'

Raven clenched his hands. Getting information out of Sarah Jane was harder than extracting teeth from an angry mountain lion.

'The storekeep told me he refused to serve her, and hinted that the orders came from Monte Grand, probably through his manager, Homer Kirk. What kind of a situation have you got around here?'

'I'd rather leave the explanations to Beth. She wouldn't thank me for butting in.'

'Find her for me, or point me into the right direction to find her myself, and I'll gladly wait for her explanation. But she could be in a bad situation right now.'

'I can't get involved in this. My father has already told me not to see Beth again.'

'And that's how your friendship works, huh?' Raven paused to consider his position, but already he was concerned about Beth and what might have happened to her.

'What about you?' Sarah Jane countered. 'You're ready to duck out at the first chance. You did accept a job with her brand, but you're going to break your word, aren't you? You have no intention of going to work for Diamond Cross.'

'I'm trying to find out what happened to her,' he rapped impatiently. 'Is there anyone else in town she might have decided to visit on impulse?'

'Not Beth. She hates the town and everyone in it.'

'That's a sweeping statement. Can you pick it to pieces a little and let me know why she's got such an attitude?'

'She doesn't know who's back of her trouble, although she reckons she's got a good idea. That's why she is so keen on getting someone of your calibre on her side. She thought your presence might smoke out the polecats. She's never found out who bushwhacked her father, and she's fighting to save the ranch. Some very bad things are happening around the county, and when the shooting starts, no one will be safe.'

'Is that why your father warned you

off seeing Beth? You run a cheap kind of friendship.'

'That isn't fair! There's nothing I can do to help her. She needs someone like you to fight her battles.'

'Gunnies come cheap for that sort of thing.' Raven considered for a few moments. There was a picture of Beth Hallam uppermost in his mind and he knew instinctively that he could not turn his back on her. There had been something about her that struck him forcibly the moment he set eyes on her. He drew a deep breath and held it until his lungs protested, then exhaled in a long, hard sigh.

'What are you going to do?' Sarah Jane was watching him intently, and seemed able to read his thoughts.

'I'll have to do it the hard way,' he said softly. 'Beth was refused service at the store, so it's likely she went to talk with the man who gave the order. That would be Homer Kirk, Monte Grand's manager. Is that right?'

Sarah Jane nodded and turned away,

intending to re-enter the bank. Raven grasped her arm.

'Not so fast. Tell me something about the set-up around here. Kirk is Grand's top man in town. Does he have a crew to do his dirty work for him?'

'About four tough gunnies who don't have to answer to the law for anything they do. That's the kind of set-up around here. I don't know about the sheriff, but Clint Jackson is crooked. He tried to get my father to pay money to have the bank watched for robbers, and it doesn't stretch the imagination to work out who is in on that.'

'Did your father pay up?'

'No. Dad is like a mule when it comes to money.'

Raven climbed into his saddle and rode back along the street to tie his mount to the rail outside Lappard's saloon. He glanced around the street, then went to the building next door, where a brass sign on the wall proclaimed that the office within belonged to Monte Grand. His spurs tinkled on the boardwalk as he crossed to the office door, and he entered to find himself in a small office which contained nothing more than a desk and two chairs. There was an inner door in the back wall, which stood ajar, and Raven could hear the sound of voices coming from an inner office. A middle-aged man in a brown store suit was seated at the desk, poring over some paperwork, and he looked up in surprise at Raven.

'The saloon is next door,' he said pointedly.

'I'm not blind; I saw the saloon.' Raven's smile was deceptively friendly. 'I want to see Homer Kirk. He's Monte Grand's top man in town, ain't he?'

'Mr Kirk is not in this morning,' the man said firmly.

'Who's in there then?'

Raven jerked his head in the direction of the inner office. He moved forward and the man sprang up and ran to the door. Raven followed closely and reached over the man's shoulder when he paused to bar the way. He thrust the inner door with the flat of his left hand and it swung open to reveal a man sitting at a big desk inside the room. Beth Hallam was seated on a chair to the right of the desk, her back to a window, and a tough-looking gunnie was standing behind the girl, a heavy hand on her shoulder to keep her in the seat.

'Homer Kirk.' Raven almost lifted the clerk bodily out of the doorway and he scuttled back to his desk. Raven strode into the office, his gaze on the seated man. The hardcase straightened and stepped back to give himself room, his right hand dropping to the butt of his holstered gun. 'Don't make the mistake of lifting your gun, fella. Just stand still until I can get around to you.'

'Who in hell are you?' Kirk sat motionless behind the desk, his hands in plain view. He was a big man, well dressed in a pale-blue store suit, a white shirt and a red tie. He was fleshy from too much sitting at the desk. His face

49

was puffy, his large nose swollen and twisted out of shape, and there was a deep scar on his left cheek that angled upwards from the corner of his mouth to the lobe of his ear. His dark eyes were deepset, and became filled with anger as he regarded Raven.

'I'm working for Diamond Cross. What are you doing with my boss? It sure looked like you were holding her pretty much against her will. You came here because you were refused service at the store, huh?' He addressed the silent girl without looking at her. 'And it's obvious that you ain't getting any satisfaction from these galoots. Ask your question again, boss, and we'll see if my presence adds weight to your words.'

'Get him outa here, Dekker,' Kirk rapped.

The hardcase reached for his gun. Raven drew and fired. The office was rocked by the heavy report of the shot. Dekker jerked under the impact of the bullet that shattered his right shoulder.

He twisted and fell heavily to the floor. Gunsmoke plumed across the big room as Raven turned his muzzle to cover the desk. Kirk had started his right hand to the hideout gun he was carrying in his left armpit.

'You ain't got a prayer.' Raven observed.

Kirk stopped his move and dropped his hand back to the desk. His eyes narrowed as he tried to gauge the speed of the draw he had witnessed. He glanced at Dekker, stretched out on his back on the floor, apparently unconscious, then returned his gaze to Raven's set features.

'OK.' He shrugged. 'You win this time. I've never seen anyone as fast as you.'

'I play for keeps.' Raven was grim-faced. 'Get rid of your gun and do it slow. Throw it on the floor.'

Kirk obeyed, then leaned back in his seat. 'You got the drop on me,' he admitted. 'But getting out of here is something else. That shot will have alerted the rest of my men, and they'll be waiting outside for you, mister. It's your move, and I'll be mighty interested in how you handle it.'

'You better start praying that I do it right, because if I don't you will be dead. Are you ready to leave, Miss Hallam?'

Beth was white-faced, but there was a glint in her eyes as she stood up. Her pistol was lying on a corner of the big desk and she picked it up and slid it into her holster.

'Let's go,' she said.

'Come on, Kirk.' Raven waggled his gun. 'You're going with us, and remember that if there's any shooting out on the street you'll be the first to draw a slug, I promise you.'

The big man's face hardened, but he got to his feet and walked to the door, his hands shoulder high. Raven followed closely, the muzzle of his deadly pistol jabbing Kirk's spine. He motioned for Beth to stay close as they left the inner office and walked to the street door.

3

Raven followed Kirk out to the sidewalk with Beth Hallam at his back. Kirk paused because a crowd was gathering on the street in front of the office. Raven noted two hard cases standing in the forefront of the knot of townsmen, hands on their holstered weapons, and guessed they were Kirk's men. He saw Clint Jackson coming almost at a run from the law office. The big deputy was carrying a double-barrelled shotgun and sunlight was glinting on his law star.

Kirk glanced at Raven, a grin on his thick lips, and Raven resisted an impulse to swipe the big man with the barrel of his Colt.

'What now?' Kirk demanded. 'It looks like stand-off.'

'I'm gonna hand you over to the law.' Raven saw Kirk's grin widen. 'If you think that's good news then take another pull at it. If Jackson doesn't do his duty I'll handle you myself. You're going to jail for holding Beth against her will.'

'And if you think you can buck Monte Grand and get away with it then you're riding the wrong horse,' Kirk countered. 'Monte runs this county with a big hand.'

'What's going on?' Jackson demanded upon arrival, glowering at Raven. 'You been causing trouble, Raven?'

'Raven?' Kirk's smile disappeared and his face took on a blend of disbelief and fear as the dreaded name sank into his mind. 'Raven, the killer? What goes on here? I would have got the word if someone like Raven was coming in. Is this another of your tricks, Jackson? Monte warned you about pulling against him. If you step outa line again you'll wake up one fine morning and find yourself dead.'

'The deputy is joking,' Raven observed. 'He thought I was Raven when I showed up in town, but he knows different or he'd have more respect for me.'

'I was refused service at the store,' Beth cut in. She was glaring at Jackson, her tone tight with anger. 'I came to see Kirk about it and he got tough with me. Drake showed up when Dekker was manhandling me. Dekker made a mistake and reached for his gun. He's lying on the floor of Kirk's office.'

A ripple of excitement tremored through the gathering crowd.

'Is she telling the truth, Kirk?' Jackson demanded. 'This is a serious charge, if it is true.'

'She came busting into my office like she owned the place, waving that fancy gun of hers, and Dekker disarmed her.' Kirk's voice sounded like he had swallowed a shovelful of creek stones. 'He was trying to quieten her down when Raven showed up, and got plugged for his efforts.'

'Dekker drew first,' Raven said. 'It was self-defence.'

'We'll leave that for the judge to decide.' Jackson lifted his shotgun until the muzzle lined up on Raven's big figure, but Raven slid behind Kirk and Jackson found himself covering the sweating manager.

'Put that gun down, you fool,' Kirk rasped. He ran a forefinger around the inside of his collar. 'If this man is Raven he could wipe out all of us while you're still wondering what to do. Get out of here, Jackson. I'll handle this.'

Jackson gazed at Kirk with dislike on his heavy features. He resented being reprimanded in front of the townsmen, and his eyes burned with an inner fire.

'This is a matter for the law,' Jackson rasped, 'and I don't need you to tell me my duty. I'll handle this so you better keep your mouth shut and let me get on with it or you might find yourself on the inside of the jail, looking out.'

Someone in the crowd guffawed and Jackson turned, waving his shotgun.

'Get the hell out of here,' he ordered.

No one moved and Jackson, suddenly

furious, turned back to Kirk. He seemed on the point of losing his patience. His knuckles showed white as he gripped the shotgun. He opened his mouth, but at that moment the sound of several horses coming along the street intervened. Raven glanced to the right to see three riders cantering into town. He heard Kirk utter an imprecation, and recognized relief in the man's tone.

The trio came on to the front of the office, scattering the dozen or so townsmen. The foremost of the three caught and held Raven's attention. He was a man of around forty-five, striking in appearance and immensely tall in the saddle. His black eyebrows were bushy. He wore black side burns, a thin black moustache, and his long, dark features hinted at mixed blood somewhere in his lineage. He was wearing a brown store suit, a black, flat-crowned Stetson, and shiny black riding boots. His horse was a big black stallion, its saddle and bridle decorated liberally with silver.

'Mr Grand, am I glad to see you!' Kirk said hurriedly. 'I've got some trouble here.'

Monte Grand gigged his horse forward until the animal's large head nudged Jackson in the face. The deputy ducked and moved on to the sidewalk, where he stood scowling at Grand. Raven's gaze flickered to the two men with Grand, and noted that they were gunslingers, alert-eyed, their hands still, close to the butts of their weapons. Both men were intent in their gaze at Raven.

'There's always something,' Grand responded. 'What is it now?'

His dark gaze was on Raven, his expression inscrutable as he took in Raven's appearance. Raven noted that Grand was not wearing a gun, and that told him much about the man. He listened while Kirk gave his boss a garbled account of what had happened in his office, and Grand listened intently until his manager lapsed into silence, his gaze never leaving Raven's angular face. Then he leaned forward slightly in his saddle and spoke in a harsh voice, his gaze intent on Raven.

'You're a stranger in town,' he said. 'What's your name? Have you got business here?'

'He's Raven, the gunman,' Jackson said quickly. 'That's who he is, no matter what he tells you.'

'I'm getting a mite tired of being called someone I ain't,' Raven said.

'Troy Batson is getting into town later today,' Jackson added. 'He's seen Raven. I'll know where I stand if he identifies you.'

'And what will you do if he is Raven?' The ghost of a smile touched Grand's lips and a ripple of derisive laughter trickled through the watching townsmen.

Jackson grimaced but did not answer. Raven's mind had fastened on the name Jackson had mentioned — Troy Batson — for he remembered Batson, a gunslinger who had come off second-best when they clashed in a range war

59

in Kansas several years before. He had heard that Batson died as a result of his wounds, but false rumours always abounded and it was possible the gunman had survived. He shrugged and addressed the deputy.

'Jackson. You can put Kirk in jail,' Raven said.

'No.' Beth spoke sharply. 'I like the way you'd handle it, Pete, but we don't need a showdown right now.' She turned her gaze to Grand, her voice filled with loathing when she addressed him. 'One of these days you'll go too far, Monte, and you'll take a fall. You better learn that you can't mess with Diamond Cross and get away with it.'

Grand smiled and stepped down from his saddle. He stood almost as tall as Raven, and came upon the wooden sidewalk to gaze into Raven's face.

'I'll pay you twice what you'll get from Diamond Cross,' he said.

'I already got a job.' Raven gave the appearance of being relaxed, but he was tense like a coiled spring. 'The trouble

Beth had this morning when she went into the store — if you're responsible, I'll kill you.'

Grand's face did not change expression. He smiled coldly. Jackson came forward, his face showing desperation.

'I want no trouble in town,' he said sharply. 'Wilson has told me to act tough. You've all been getting away with too much and it's got to stop.'

'Get lost,' Grand said. 'Don't get too big for your boots, Jackson. You can lose that badge you're wearing. Go do your yapping someplace else.'

'You can't talk to me like that.' Jackson's face reddened at the lash in Grand's tone.

'Beat it, Jackson,' Raven said.

'I — ' Jackson started to say more but changed his mind. He lifted the twin muzzles of his shotgun, then shrugged and lowered them again.

Raven watched as Jackson turned on his heel. The deputy's boots rapped sullenly on the sidewalk as he retired to the law office.

'He believes you're Raven.' Grand observed.

'And you don't?' Raven countered.

'I think there's a good chance you are the killer. Beth has been trying to locate Raven for weeks, and suddenly you turn up out of the blue. I've got a gunhand coming to join my crew who knows Raven, and he'll settle the matter of your identity. Ever heard of Stig Ivey?'

'Ivey is an outlaw, not a gunhand.' Raven's features remained expressionless but his mind whirled at the mention of the gang boss who had shot down his mother and brother.

'No one dares tell him that to his face.' Grand smiled. 'What are you going to do about Kirk?'

'He can accompany us to the store and tell Meagher he's changed his mind about refusing service to Diamond Cross. Have you got any objection?'

Grand shook his head. 'I'll be in the office when you get back, Kirk.'

He turned on his heel and entered the building. Kirk started along the sidewalk without being told and Raven followed him. Beth hurried to stay with Raven and they went to the store.

Meagher said nothing when Kirk relayed the situation to him. Kirk turned to Raven.

'Is that all?' He had an arrogant way of talking and again Raven was tempted to hit him.

'I'll let you know if I think of anything else,' Raven told him. 'Don't push your luck, Kirk.'

Kirk departed. Raven walked to the door to peer around the street. He saw Kirk hurrying back to his office. Jackson was standing in front of the law office. Raven went back to Beth, and waited in the background while she made some small purchases. Jackson came into the store, still carrying his shotgun. He did not speak although his expression showed that he was far from happy with the situation.

'We'll ride out to the ranch now,' Beth decided. 'Then we'll make plans on how to beat the crooked set-up around here.'

Raven followed the girl out to the street. Until he heard Grand mention Stig Ivey he had been determined to quit the instant he got Beth alone to tell her, but mention of the outlaw had changed his mind in a hurry. He fetched his horse from the front of the bank and they rode out of town. Raven heaved a long sigh when they reached the open trail.

'I'm so glad you came in response to the feelers I put out for you,' Beth said.

'I'm not happy about that,' he growled. 'I was living a quiet life in Mexico until you started a barn dance in my back yard, making those enquiries about my whereabouts. I had to kill a bounty hunter who came looking for me, and the Rurales began to show an interest. I came to tell you to lay off. I had quit the gun trail and was trying to settle down, but you made it impossible for me to stay below the border.'

'Are you going to quit on me now?'

Raven glanced sideways at her, then shook his head, his dark eyes filled with resolution. The mention of Stig Ivey's imminent arrival had settled the question of his immediate future.

'No. Grand mentioned a name that interested me. I'll stick around until I can get a bead on Stig Ivey.'

'What's Ivey done to you?'

'How far is it to Diamond Cross?'

Beth sighed, and a sadness came to her face that was reflected in her eyes.

'I'm sorry for any trouble I've put you to.' Her voice trembled. 'I was at the end of my rope. My father had been shot down and was lying at death's door. I could hear the wolves baying for blood — Hallam blood — and I was alone in my fight to save Diamond Cross. I was really desperate when I hit on the idea of enlisting your aid. I thought that if I offered you enough money you'd come running. I didn't think it through like I should have, and I just didn't think my efforts might have put you in a bad situation.'

'Forget about it,' he advised. 'You might have done me a big favour at that. I looked for Stig Ivey a long time before I decided to cross the border into Mexico. Ivey had vanished without trace until Grand mentioned him back there in town.'

'The lure of big money has attracted him. All the bad men in the West are heading in this direction, it seems, and Diamond Cross looks to be their target.'

They rode at a comfortable jog across the seemingly deserted plain. In the distance a range of mountains shimmered in the heat haze. The intense silence seemed to have the throbbing beat of menace in its very fabric.

Raven did not relax his habitual caution. He was aware that yet again he was being denied the refuge for which he had long sought, as if the unknown Fates had earmarked him for the inevitable end that attended men of his ilk. He was already embroiled in the trouble dogging Diamond Cross, and by taking Beth's part against Monte Grand he had aligned himself against the force set up by the girl's enemies. If he did not depart immediately he would be inextricably snared in the turmoil that abounded, and deserving of whatever trouble might ensue, for he realized that there could be no going back once he crossed that point of no return.

His dark gaze was keenly aware of their surroundings, and he watched for signs of human presence among the natural features through which they passed. Once he thought he heard the distant sound of pounding hoofs to the right rear, and twisted in his jolting saddle to listen keenly. It sounded as if someone riding out from town was intent on passing them unseen, but he saw nothing and faced his front.

Later, he caught the glint of sunlight on metal off to their right and reached out a big hand to grasp Beth by the shoulder and haul her out of leather.

She uttered a cry of shock as she was plucked from her saddle and dragged across Raven's mount to fall with his swiftly moving body as he hurled himself sideways to the hard ground. He landed with an impact that drove the breath from his body, and as she fell upon him the crash of a rifle shot hammered and echoed.

Raven pushed her roughly into cover and lifted his Colt from its holster.

'Stay down,' he rapped, and she lay motionless, listening to the fading echoes of the shot, her eyes widening when she saw blood staining his left sleeve above the elbow.

'You've been hit!' she gasped, and struggled to sit up.

Raven held her down with a heavy hand. He was peering in the direction from which the shot had come. There was a puff of gunsmoke drifting on the hot breeze around the spot where he had seen the metallic glint, and it was out of range of his pistol. He glanced towards his horse, but his Winchester was out of reach. He flattened out a little and lay watching.

'Stay down,' he commanded when Beth tried to push herself up.

'You're bleeding,' she rapped. 'Let me take a look at your wound.'

'It won't kill me, but the next shot might. Do as you're told. Leave it be.'

He saw a faint movement from the spot where the ambusher had fired, and caught a glimpse of the high crown of a sombrero moving back into deeper cover. He sprang up, lunged towards his horse and snatched his Winchester from its scabbard. Again the hidden rifle cracked, sending a bullet to snarl in his ear as he threw himself flat. He worked the mechanism of his rifle and jacked a 44.40 cartridge into the breech. The rifle covered the ambush position, and he fired instantly when he saw further movement.

Echoes rolled across the range. He saw the ambusher jerk under the impact of the slug, and the sombrero showed briefly again. As it rose above its cover, Raven fired once more, and a pang of satisfaction stabbed through him when the hat disappeared abruptly.

He stood up slowly, rifle ready for further action, but nothing happened. The gun echoes were growling away into the vast distance. Beth sprang up and grasped his left elbow, but Raven shook her off, refusing to let her distract him.

'Stay down until I've checked out the ambusher,' he growled, irritated by her lack of fear under fire.

He went to his horse and swung into the saddle, ignoring the pain in his left arm, his gaze fixed upon the ambush spot. He sent the horse forward at a lope, rifle ready, and reined in when he could see a man sprawled in cover with a discarded rifle lying nearby. He dismounted and trailed his reins, then went forward on foot until he could look down upon the hard features of the man who had ambushed them.

The ambusher was dead with a bullet hole in the front of his tall sombrero and a slug through his forehead. Blood was staining his rough features. Raven remained still until Beth arrived. The girl slid from her saddle and came to stand beside him, unmoved by the sight of the dead man.

'Do you know him?' Raven demanded.

'Never seen him before. He's just another stranger brought in to make things tough for Diamond Cross. Shall we take him on to the ranch?'

Raven shook his head. 'Leave him for the buzzards. He was meant to be crowbait from the day he was born. Let's get on to your place, and you can tell me about the men on your payroll. Why has your foreman set two gunnies to watch you? Is he expecting something bad to happen to you?'

'Not Ham Sheridan. He hasn't got a decent bone in his body. My father sets great store by Sheridan but I don't like him. He's as bad as the hard cases who are out to cause trouble for us. He's the one who insists on hiring gunhands.'

'Did he know you were trying to

contact me?' Raven watched her intently as they resumed their ride to the ranch.

'I never let my left hand know what my right hand is doing,' she said with a shake of her head. 'Also, I have no idea who is for or against me. This trouble started a long time ago. It's only now that it has reached these impossible proportions. Rustling started about this time last year, and it isn't only Diamond Cross suffering losses. Sheridan doesn't seem able to cope despite his abilities. He hasn't caught one rustler.'

'Put me on the job of stopping the rustlers and I'll get good results.'

'The job is yours.' Relief sounded in Beth's tone. 'Shall we talk about wages? With your reputation, I expect you'll come pretty high.'

'Forget about money. If I get to face Stig Ivey I'll pay you for the privilege. We'll play the game as the cards fall, huh?'

'No.' Her tone was firm. 'I've

72

disrupted your life and I expect to pay for that.'

'So let's talk about it later,' he responded.

It was during late afternoon when Beth reined up and they both gazed intently into the valley that had opened its vista before them.

'This is Diamond Cross,' Beth said proudly.

Ridges that were thickly timbered filled the skyline around the valley. The late afternoon sun marked the course of a wide stream with glinting reflections. A huddled group of log buildings surrounded a much larger ranch house, and there were three corrals in the background. Horses aplenty inhabited the corrals, and a number of men were busy around the spread.

'Your father picked his spot well,' Raven observed.

'And Monte Grand means to take it away from him.' Her tone reflected the harshness of her thoughts.

Raven glanced at her set features. She

was clutching her reins tightly, her knuckles showing white. Raven sighed inaudibly, aware that he was caught up in this grim situation. Something about Beth Hallam touched a hidden nerve inside him and he knew it would be useless trying to break free of the invisible net she had cast about him.

'Do you have any proof that Grand is responsible?' His voice was low-pitched. 'I'm not interested in supposition or intuition. Just give me plain facts.'

'Of course there is no evidence.' She shook her head and hopelessness sounded in her voice. Her slim shoulders slumped. 'Whoever is responsible is too cute to be caught out. Sure it looks like Grand is back of it. He's got the town in the palm of his hand, and Kirk wouldn't have told Meagher not to serve me unless Grand said so.'

She gigged her mount and started down the trail into the valley. Raven glanced around, checking their back trail, then followed her closely. He was getting used to the knowledge that his future was uncertain again, as in the old days, and he wanted to finish this fight as quickly as possible, aware that Beth's enemies would strike at him without warning. He knew they could not take chances with a man of his reputation. Already one attempt had been made against him, and he knew the next would be more carefully plotted.

He rode into Diamond Cross with death at his shoulder and in his holster, prepared to risk everything for the woman beside him.

4

Beth glanced at Raven as they entered the yard at Diamond Cross. Her expression showed that she was under great strain. Raven wondered at her thoughts. His gaze flitted across the scene before them, noting an armed guard standing in the open doorway of the barn and another leaning in the loft doorway above.

'How many men on the payroll?' He spoke sharply, wanting to distract her from her thoughts.

'Eighteen, including four gunnies.'

'And those four include the two who escorted you into town?'

'Yes. Sheridan has been handling them. He insists that two guards are always on watch around the yard. Some of the smaller spreads in the county have been raided — shot up and burned.'

'I'll take over the defence of the spread.'

'As well as hunting down the rustlers?' She searched his face as if looking for answers to a host of questions that she could not put into words, and then nodded. 'Sure. OK. I can tell Sheridan now. He's coming out to meet us.'

Raven had already spotted the rider cantering towards them across the yard, and his lips pulled tight as he took in the ramrod's appearance. Ham Sheridan was a big man, tight-lipped, his prominent nose a thin ridge separating his mouth from narrowed, purposeful eyes. He was tall and heavily built, solid and hard, with powerful arms and large, ham-like hands. Dusty range garb was stretched over his massive figure — blue denim trousers and jacket, narrow shotgun chaps, and the brim of his black Stetson was pulled low over his hard gaze. A black gunbelt buckled around his heavy waist had the bone-handled butt of a .45 Colt protruding from the scuffed holster. He looked to be in his early forties, Raven judged. He looked arrogant, and the gleam in his eyes indicated a raw temperament.

Sheridan reined up in front of them, blocking their way, and Raven smiled, guessing that the two riders he dismissed in town had returned to report to the foreman.

'Who's this?' Sheridan's voice rasped deep in his chest. 'Another stray dog you've picked up? I've told you to leave the hiring and firing to me, Beth. I run this outfit and I like to do it my way. Bringing in a gunnie you met in town might be taking on more trouble instead of easing the situation. He could be one of Grand's men, sent in to work under cover.' His harsh gaze burned into Raven. 'You better turn that hoss and ride out of here. I don't need another gun at this time.'

'Stop that, Ham. I've hired Pete and he's staying. He's going to take over the job you set Hibbert and Gadson to do.

I've had enough of their company.'

'And this fella can do the job better, huh?' Sheridan shook his head. 'I don't think so, and what I say goes around here. Get moving, Bo, before I throw you outa the yard.'

'I guess you must be hard of hearing.' Raven's eyes were narrowed but his voice was smooth, his tone gentle. He grinned derisively as dull colour seeped into the foreman's face. 'I'm hired, and I ain't no ordinary ranch hand. You can't give orders to me. I answer only to the boss, and the sooner you get that under your bonnet the better.'

Sheridan's thin lips pulled tight and the gleam in his eyes turned into a red flame. Raven touched spurs to his horse and the animal surged forward, bearing down on Sheridan's dun. The foreman jerked on his reins, twitching his mount clear to avoid being run down. Astonishment showed briefly on Beth's face, but she followed Raven closely and they continued towards the ranch house. Raven did not look around at

Sheridan, but heard the hoofs of the man's horse rattle on the hard-packed dirt of the yard as he came along behind.

'I'm surprised at you, Pete,' Beth said softly. 'You've antagonized Sheridan and I would have thought you'd try to make friends with him. Why did you do that? We don't need friction among the crew.'

'I need to find out exactly what kind of a man he is, and this is the best way of handling it. The ranch foreman is the man who makes the wheels go round, and if a situation doesn't improve then he's to blame. If your trouble has worsened like you say it has then it's all down to Sheridan, and he's got to answer for that.'

They reached the porch and Raven dismounted swiftly, turning to face Sheridan as the foreman came up. Sheridan's face was livid, his eyes blazing with anger. Raven tensed, ready for trouble, but Sheridan reined in, the nose of his mount almost touching Beth as she slid out of her saddle. She grasped Sheridan's bridle and pushed the horse away.

'Let's have this out now, Beth,' Sheridan growled. 'You've been spoiling for a fight with me for weeks.'

'Yeah, you're right, ever since my father was shot, which proved to me that you weren't doing your job properly. Since the ambush I've been watching you. You've been going through the motions of doing your duties, but nothing definite ever gets done. I don't know what's in your mind, Ham, but whatever it is, I don't like it.'

'I've bent over backwards doing my job,' Sheridan snarled. 'Is this all the thanks I get? I ain't got eyes in the back of my head and I can't be in more than one place at a time. If we had twice as many gunnies we wouldn't be able to cover everything, and I've been telling you that for as long as I can remember. Now you bring in this jasper, and he's nothing but trouble. If you think you've got problems now then wait until he starts throwing his weight around. What do you want me to do, huh? Quit? That's what you're asking for. I ain't gonna take much more of trying to do my job with you acting the big boss. A foreman has to have control, but you've got that, and you've been changing my orders without even talking to me about it. Well I'm ready to up stakes and haul my freight. I've had a bellyful.'

'If you can't work with me then you'd better leave.' Beth's eyes glinted with fury as she drew a deep breath. 'Why are you making a big play right now, Ham? Is it because I brought Pete in? You didn't like me sending Hibbert and Gadson back to the ranch, huh? Is that what's behind this?'

'You know it ain't safe any more for you to be riding around the range alone. How many times I got to tell you that? You're playing right into Grand's hands. He's only got to drop on to you in some lonely spot and it will be all up with Diamond Cross. With you out of the way and your Pa helpless, the spread will go to pieces. I ain't gonna struggle on any longer. I quit.'

'But you'd stay if I sent Pete packing, is that it?' Beth wrapped her reins around the hitching rail, then ascended the porch steps. Raven was watching her closely. She seemed to have reached the end of her tether as she sighed heavily. 'OK, Ham, if that's what's in your mind. Come into the office and I'll give you your time.'

'It'll be a pleasure.' Sheridan glared at Raven and stepped up on to the porch.

'Come along, Pete,' Beth said quickly. 'From now on you're to shadow me. I'll run things the way they should be done. I'll want more gunnies on the payroll, and we'll hit the rustlers hard if they venture on to Diamond Cross.'

Raven was puzzling over Sheridan's attitude. He could not understand why the ramrod had quit. He followed Beth into the ranch office and stood in the background while the girl paid off her foreman. Sheridan took the wad of notes Beth thrust at him and departed without a word. His boots thudded on the porch, the sound echoing through the house. A moment later hoofs pounded as Sheridan departed.

'I don't know what got into Ham,' Beth said unsteadily. 'But he hasn't been himself for a long time. It must be the strain of working under pressure. But him quitting like that has put me out on a limb. I can put Buck Fuller in charge of the ranch, but he's no gunman and couldn't handle that kind of a crew. The wage bill is terribly high now, but we can do with more gunmen.'

'I thought you got me up from Mexico to handle your fight?' Raven challenged.

'I'm having second thoughts about that right now. It's such a responsible job, trying to fight a crooked set-up. No wonder Ham quit.'

As Raven opened his mouth to reply

the report of a rifle shot hammered and then echoed. He spun on his heel and ran out to the porch, calling to Beth to remain under cover when he heard her following closely. He paused in the doorway and looked around. Gun echoes were fading sullenly into the distance. He saw an inert figure lying in the yard, and the men who had been working around the spread were no longer in sight.

Beth pushed impatiently against Raven but he refused to move out of the doorway.

'What's happened?' She demanded.

'You've got a dead man in the yard.' Raven's eyes hardened when a second shot crackled. He heard a bullet strike the wall some two inches from his head and slid back into cover. 'Has this happened before?'

'No.' Beth gazed at him with the sparkle of fear in her dark eyes.

'Stay inside the house while I take a look around, and this time do like I tell you. If you make a habit of disobeying me when lead is flying I'll be the next one to quit.'

She opened her mouth to reply, then closed it and compressed her lips. Raven smiled grimly.

'It hurts you to take orders, huh? Well you better start learning how to do it or you'll make my job harder than it should be.'

She nodded wordlessly and turned away, moving to the staircase and ascending quickly. Raven peered out the doorway again. Two riders were hammering across the yard towards the gate, intent on locating the sniper. Raven went out to the porch and crossed the yard to the barn, where several of the crew were standing in a tight group around the dead ranch hand.

'We can't do anything for him,' an oldish, bearded man was saying as Raven paused. He turned and looked questioningly at Raven. 'Who are you? I saw you ride in with Miz Beth.'

'She hired me in town. I'm gonna

fight the rustlers.'

A silence ensued while the half dozen men considered Raven, noting his appearance and manner.

'You got a name?' The old man asked.

'Pete Drake.'

'That's the name Gadson mentioned when he rode in from town,' someone said. 'Him and Hibbert came back with their tails between their legs talking about the fastest draw they'd ever seen. Hibbert was white-faced. Said a man called Pete Drake shot his hat off his head from an even break and had the drop on him before Hibbert cleared leather.'

'Where is Hibbert now?' Raven asked.

'Quit cold. Collected his pay, went straight to the bunkhouse, grabbed his gear, and raised dust out of here.'

'Where's Gadson?' Raven persisted.

The old man moved aside. His blocky figure had been covering the dead man from Raven's gaze. Raven looked closely at the inert body and recognized him as one of the pair who had escorted Beth to town.

'That's Gadson. I'm Buck Fuller. Is it true Sheridan has quit?'

'Sure. Didn't you see him ride out?'

'The shot that killed Gadson came from the spot where Sheridan rode out of sight,' Fuller said. 'Looks like he settled an old score, huh?'

The gathered men mumbled agreement. Several others were beginning to drift out of concealment and came to the spot where Gadson was lying. Raven stirred impatiently.

'I've been hired to run the gun crew,' he said. 'Fuller, you better go over to the house and see Beth. Who's carrying guns for the spread?'

'We're all ready to fight for the brand,' Fuller said. 'But Henker and Mason are the only two drawing gun wages now Gadson is dead and Hibbert has quit, and they rode out fast when the shooting started. If they catch up with the sniper they'll bring him back dead. Charlie, throw Gadson across a saddle and take him into town. His body will give Jackson something to think about. The rest of you get on with your chores. Bunching up like this ain't good. You're asking for trouble, and that is what we've got a lot of on this range.'

Raven turned back towards the house and Fuller accompanied him.

'I heard tell that Miz Beth rode into town to meet Raven, the gunman,' Fuller said.

'That's what I heard,' Raven agreed, and Fuller glanced at him.

'Are you Raven?'

'They say I look like him. Jackson, the deputy, went a step further. He wanted to arrest me as Raven.'

'What changed his mind?'

'Raven's reputation, I guess.'

They reached the house and Beth came out to the porch. Her face was set in harsh lines, her eyes hard and cold.

'Buck, will you take over Sheridan's job?' She demanded.

'Sure thing, but only if it lets me get

on with ranch business. I ain't a gunnie.'

'You won't have to worry about that. Pete will take care of the shooting. He's pretty good at it. All you'll have to do is run the everyday things and keep the ranch hands busy. That's a full-time job, and it's yours if you want it.'

'I'll take it on,' Fuller glanced curiously at Raven. 'You'd need to be Raven hisself to make any impression on the trouble we got around here. But you can count on the whole outfit if it comes to a showdown. We'll all fight for the brand. What we've needed is someone who can lead us.'

'Good. I reckon there'll be a lot of fighting to do.' Raven looked at Beth as Fuller departed, trying to gauge the degree of her determination. 'You seem certain that Monte Grand is behind your trouble. Do you have any proof? I wouldn't want to act on hearsay. That would bring the law down on you before I managed to fire a couple of shots. Is there anyone in the county you can point to with the sure knowledge that they are committed against you?'

'I don't even know who shot my father.' She shook her head, and for a moment hopelessness showed in her expression. Then she stiffened and seemed to take a fresh grip on her emotions. 'You're gonna have to handle this from the bottom up, Pete. You'll have to find the man responsible.'

'I won't be able to do that if I sit around here waiting for him to tip his hand.' He thrust out his bottom lip as he considered. 'I guess the obvious place to start looking for the bad men is the ambush that got your father. Has he said anything about it?'

'He never saw a thing. He was shot in the back from cover. You can talk to him if you like. He's confined to his bed, making my life a misery as if it's my fault he's on his back. If I didn't throw myself into this fight I think I might quit, but that's a luxury I can't afford. I went to the scene of the ambush the day after it happened and looked around. I found the spot where the ambusher waited. He must have seen Pa in town and planned to kill him on his way back to the ranch. I didn't find anything to point me in the direction of the ambusher, and after the sheriff came out to look around he formed the same opinion.'

'It shouldn't be too difficult to get a line on the men against you,' he mused. 'From what I've seen so far, Monte Grand is in there somewhere, and his manager, Homer Kirk. All I have to do is watch one or the other for a few days, and if they are making trouble for you I should see some signs of it. You'll have to spare me for that chore, and I'll ride out at once.'

Beth's face expressed disfavour as she shook her head.

'Now you're here I feel I can't do without you. There must be some other way.'

'My way is the easiest and the quickest. You'll just have to go along with what I say. I'm gonna run the job my way, and if you don't like it you got one of two choices.'

'What are they?'

'Agree with me or fire me.' He grinned. 'There ain't no other way. So what's it to be?'

'You don't have to bully me,' she responded. 'Do it your way.' She shrugged and turned away. 'You'll report back to me if you get on to something, won't you?'

'If I find anything I'll push it through to a conclusion before coming back to you,' he replied. 'I'll stick around until Henker and Mason get back. I need to know what they find out there.'

'I can hear hoofs now,' Beth said. 'They're coming back.'

They walked out to the porch. Two riders were coming in at the gate and making for the house. Raven studied them as they came up, aware that they were missing no detail about his appearance. One man was tall and thin, his face long and angular. His manner suggested a man who was living on his nerves. He was wearing twin Colts holstered around his waist on sagging belts, and many brass cartridges gleamed in the loops on the belts. The other man was shorter, heavier in build, with a round face and hard brown eyes. They reined up at the edge of the porch in a rapidly rising cloud of dust.

'Well?' Beth's voice was tight with anticipation. 'What did you find, Henker?'

'It wasn't Sheridan,' the tall rider said. 'We figured it was when we rode out because him and Gadson never hit it off. But Sheridan's tracks headed towards town, and we had to ride in the opposite direction. We found the spot where the shots were fired from, and followed tracks until we lost them in the rocks on the west rim. We hunted around for a spell but that killer looked like he sprouted wings and flew back to where he came from so we didn't get a line on him.'

'You're Henker, huh?' Raven queried, and the tall man nodded.

'I'm Mason,' the other said needlessly. 'Who in hell are you, stranger?'

'He's Pete Drake, the new gun boss,' Beth said. 'You'll be taking all your orders from him in future.'

Both men eyed Raven silently, and he grinned.

'One of you can show me where you found the tracks of the killer,' he said.

'Mason can go,' Henker said. 'My horse pulled up favouring his left hind hoof.'

'Sure thing,' Mason nodded. 'You ready to ride now, Drake?'

Raven nodded and went to his horse, tightened the cinch and swung into the saddle. He reined the animal about and smiled at Beth.

'I'll follow the killer's tracks until I catch up with him,' he said. 'It may be some time before I get back.'

'Good luck,' she responded.

'I told you there ain't no tracks beyond the rim,' Henker said fiercely. 'You ain't taking my word for it?

Mister, that's the same as calling me a liar!'

'Is that how you see it?' Raven shrugged. 'Sounds like you got a chip on your shoulder. If I call you a liar I'll use plain language, and you'll know what I mean. Right now I'm meaning that I'm a better than average tracker, and should be able to figure out tracks better than you. Do you have a problem with that?'

Henker shook his head and stepped down from his saddle. He bent over the left hindleg of his horse and checked it. Raven turned his horse and rode towards the gate, followed by Mason, and they left the ranch. Mason urged his mount into the lead and rode at a fast clip across the valley floor, making for the stream flowing through the centre.

'I seem to know your face, Drake,' Mason said as they splashed through the fast-flowing water and continued to the side of the valley. 'I never met you before, so I must have seen a picture of you somewhere — like on a Wanted dodger.'

'I'm not wanted by the law.' Raven smiled. 'Show me the spot where the sniper fired from.'

Mason rode on to halt eventually in a stand of oak and alder. He pointed to a spot in the undergrowth that had been trampled. Raven saw a brass rifle cartridge glinting in the sunlight and stepped down from his saddle to retrieve it. He looked down the slope towards the ranch and nodded. The sniper had picked himself a good spot. He looked around, saw boot tracks going up the slope to the rim of the valley, and regained his saddle to follow. Mason stayed back.

There was hard, rock-strewn ground up beyond the rim, and Raven looked around at the lie of the land. Mason came up and reined in.

'How long have you worked for Diamond Cross?' Raven asked.

'Two years.'

'Heard of a man called Stig Ivey?'

'The word is that Ivey is coming into the county.'

'Where did you hear that?'

'Around.' Mason shrugged.

'So what's going on around here?'

'The signs are that Monte Grand is grabbing up everything of value.'

'And Diamond Cross is next on his list?'

'Sure looks like it. There ain't much around here to stop him.'

'I'm here now, and that will make a big difference.'

'I don't think so.' Mason shook his head.

'And you're content to carry a gun for the losing side, huh?' Raven grimaced. 'I don't buy that, Mason. A man in our business won't hire out to a loser. We both know that for a fact, don't we?'

'It didn't look like Diamond Cross would get dragged into this when I came on the payroll. It became obvious after I'd taken pay, and then it was too late for me to move on.'

'Yeah.' Raven nodded. 'That's how it goes. What happened when the boss was ambushed? You must have checked it out.'

'I didn't get the chance to look around. Sheridan handled that. He did a lot of things that didn't make sense. I got it figured that he was working against the brand instead of for it.'

'And you did nothing about it? Where's your loyalty? Sheridan didn't pay your wages.'

'It wouldn't have helped anyone had I reported what I thought. Sheridan would have had me out on my ear.'

'Yeah, well I reckon I'll be seeing Sheridan again, and pretty soon. Let's ride on. We got tracks to follow.'

'But there ain't no tracks.' Mason shook his head. 'You reckon you can see tracks in these rocks?'

'Just follow me.' Raven rode on, watching the ground intently, looking not at the rocks but checking the ground around them. He saw faint marks of hoofs here and there

— enough to lead him on until they left the belt of rocks behind and found easier range. Mason sat his mount then, watching Raven quartering and circling for tracks.

Raven found a set of tracks moving off to the west and signalled for Mason to join him. The gunman nodded when he saw the tracks, and respect showed in his eyes.

'I wouldn't have believed it possible if I hadn't seen it for myself,' he said. 'I reckon you could track a fish through water.'

'What lies in the direction they're heading?' Raven asked.

Mason gazed off into the distance along the line of tracks. He shook his head.

'I guess we better follow them,' he opined. 'Monte Grand's Big G is out that way, mebbe fifteen miles, but the tracks could turn off.'

'Let's get to it then.' Raven pushed his horse forward and they settled into a mile-eating lope, riding into the west.

Above them the sun was reaching down for the horizon. Raven increased his pace. He wanted to get to grips with the trouble confronting Diamond Cross, and hoped to learn something before darkness came.

A development came in the shape of a rifle bullet. Mason gasped and fell out of his saddle as the crack of the shot hammered out the silence and sent a string of racketing echoes across the desolate range. Raven kicked his feet out of his stirrups, grabbed the butt of his Winchester, and dived groundwards with the long gun in his hand as a second shot whined perilously close to his head.

5

Raven peered around for the position of the ambusher as the heavy echoes faded and an uneasy silence returned. He saw gunsmoke drifting from a rise ahead, jacked a brass cartridge into the breech of his Winchester, and waited for further movement.

'Mason, are you OK?' He called urgently, for there was no sound or movement from the gunman.

Mason did not reply. Raven maintained his concentration. He lay stretched out, his keen gaze watching the ground ahead. Shadows were creeping in around him, cutting down his range of vision. Presently, he heard hoofs pounding and lifted his rifle. The next moment four riders appeared on the rise and came galloping down towards him. Pistols began to hammer and bullets slammed into the ground around Raven's position.

He aimed his rifle, unmindful of the slugs splattering around him like deadly rain, and, working the mechanism rapidly, opened fire on the riders. The noise of his shooting rang out in a drum-roll of deafening noise. He shifted aim after each fast shot, and before the advancing riders had covered more than a few yards their saddles were emptied and the horses came on riderless.

Raven's lips were pulled tight against his teeth as he waited, his nostrils filled with the stink of burned powder. The crashing echoes of the shooting faded quickly. The horses galloped past his position and he watched the inert figures sprawled on the slope. He switched his gaze to the original ambush spot but saw no movement there. Moments later, one of the four downed riders began to move jerkily, and Raven watched him struggling up the slope until he disappeared from sight.

Twisting around, Raven looked for Mason, and his keen eyes narrowed when he saw the gunman lying sprawled on his back, arms outflung as if dead. A trickle of blood was showing on Mason's forehead, running from under his Stetson. Raven pushed himself to his feet, eyes probing ahead, anticipating another drygulch shot, but nothing untoward happened and he went to Mason's side and bent over the gunman. He was surprised to find Mason alive and removed the man's hat to reveal a gory furrow angling through the hairline. Mason was beginning to regain his senses, and Raven left him, went to his horse and swung into the saddle.

He rode up the rise and reined in by the three downed gunmen. The unknown trio were plainly dead and he did not dismount. Going on, he topped the rise and found the fourth gunman lying inert on the hard ground. He stepped down beside the crumpled figure. The man was unconscious with a bullet through his chest.

Raven tended the wound. There was hardly any blood flow and he tore a strip from the man's shirt and made a pad for the wound. The gunman opened his eyes as Raven straightened. Raven squatted back on his heels and regarded the pale face in the growing darkness.

'You're gonna die unless you get to a doctor,' Raven said softly. 'You want to tell me who you are and how you came to be shooting at me?'

'I got nothing to say,' the man mumbled.

'Suit yourself. It's your choice. Tell me what I want to know and I'll take you to Diamond Cross, where you'll be tended. Clam up on me and I'll leave you here. If I do that you'll be dead come morning.'

'You wouldn't leave me!'

Raven straightened. He went to his horse and stepped up into the saddle, moving away without so much as a second glance at the wounded man. He had covered several yards before the man called out to him.

'OK. You win. I'll spill the beans.'

Raven returned to the man's side, dismounted and trailed his reins.

'I'm listening,' he said.

'Where are the rest of my sidekicks?'

'Dead.'

'You killed them all?'

'Yeah. That makes you the lucky one.' The man was silent for a few moments. Raven dropped to one knee beside him. The darkness was almost complete and he could barely see the man's face.

'OK. Give,' Raven prompted.

'I'm Shank Moran.' The rustler's voice was listless, laced with pain. 'Me and the others work for Rafter B.'

'Rafter B. That's Floyd Buxton's place, huh? From what I heard Beth Hallam say, Buxton is not against her.'

'Buxton's as much a victim as the Hallams. Rafter B was cleaned out by rustlers a month ago. It's only a small ranch, and it looked like the rustlers were preparing to move in on the bigger ranchers by taking out the smaller spreads first. Buxton figured to get his own back. He planned to rob the bigger ranches until he got what he had lost.'

'Did Buxton find out who rustled his stock?' Raven demanded. 'Monte Grand rides the big saddle in this county, I've heard.'

'All the signs pointed to Diamond Cross. The rustled stock headed this way from Rafter B.'

'Buxton reckoned Beth Hallam stole his cattle?' Raven was surprised.

'That's what it looked like. We ran off some cattle from Monte Grand's Big G a week ago, and were coming to take a herd from Diamond Cross. Buxton reckoned to set the two ranches fighting each other. He planned to draw the gunnies from Diamond Cross by shooting up the spread and ambushing the crew when they came out to fight, then steal cattle.'

'Sounds like Buxton is an almighty desperate man. But he shouldn't have gone off half-cocked. Why didn't he report his cattle losses to the local law?'

'If you knew the local lawmen you wouldn't ask that question.'

Moran tried to sit up, groaned and fell back unconscious. The sound of a rider coming up the slope caught Raven's ears and he turned as Mason appeared. The gunman was sagging in his saddle, his left hand to his head.

'Over here, Mason.' Raven called.

Mason halted and looked around, then turned his horse and came forward through the gathering shadows.

'What in hell happened?' He slid out of his saddle, reeling slightly. 'There are three dead men back there. Who have you got there?'

Raven straightened. He could see Mason was unsteady, bewildered by his head wound.

'Take it easy,' he advised. 'Just take a look at this man and tell me who he is.'

Mason came close and bent forward to look at the man. He fell to his knees and propped himself up by leaning his weight on his splayed hands.

'Heck, it's Shank Moran,' Mason observed. 'Rafter B rider. Did you shoot him?'

'He was shooting at us.' Raven grasped Mason's left arm and helped him to his feet. He repeated what Moran had told him.

Mason cursed. 'Buxton didn't strike me as a fool,' he observed. 'What happens now?'

'We ride back to Diamond Cross with Moran. How you feeling?'

'I'm OK.' Mason turned to his horse and almost lost his balance.

Raven bent over Moran, who was unconscious, and shook his head.

'I reckon he'll die if we try to move him on a horse,' he mused. 'We'd better leave him here and send a buckboard. Trouble is, if we do that he'll be dead come morning.'

'What do you want from me?' Mason demanded. 'Sympathy?'

Raven climbed into his saddle and they headed back to Diamond Cross.

By the time they spotted the lights of the spread, Mason was back to normal. As they entered the yard a voice challenged them from the shadows and Mason replied. Raven headed for the house, and insisted that Mason accompany him when the gunman wanted to go to the cook shack. Dense shadows filled the yard and, as they reined up in front of the porch, Beth called out to them.

'I'm so glad you're back. What happened out there?'

'What makes you think something happened?' Raven swung out of his saddle.

'You wouldn't be back now if you hadn't found something,' Beth retorted.

'We were ambushed.' Raven kept out of the light issuing from the big front window and stepped up on to the porch. 'Mason took a scalp wound and he's been pretty badly shaken up.'

'Come into the house and let me take a look at you, Mason.'

Beth stood up from the rocking chair

110

she occupied and passed through the shaft of light lying across the porch. A rifle cracked from somewhere out in the darkness, and Raven heard a slug pass closely by his head before smacking into the front wall of the house. He moved instantly, grasping Beth's arm and jerking her through the doorway and into cover. A second shot hammered and the bullet struck the front of the house. Dull echoes fled away across the illimitable range.

'You've got to accept that trouble is building up fast,' Raven said. 'That means not making a target of yourself, keeping away from windows, and no lights after dark.'

Mason spoke from the doorway. 'The gun flashes showed about two hundred yards out, about where the shot that killed Gadson came from. Want me to go see what I can find?'

'No.' Raven was certain. 'You couldn't do any good out there before morning, but I'll go out alone. It seems to me that ambush spot is getting mighty popular. I reckon it should be covered by me. Mason, if you're feeling up to it then you better cover the house until daylight.'

'Sure. No one will get in here.'

Beth protested as Raven went to the door but he shook his head and went out into the night. He mounted and rode to the gate, pausing beside the guard, an anonymous shadow in the darkness.

'Did you see anything when the shots were fired?' Raven enquired.

'They came from across the stream about the spot where the shot that killed Gadson came from.'

'That's what we figure. I'm going out to look around. I won't be back before daylight. If you hear any shooting out there then ignore it. I'll be covering the area.'

He rode out and picked his way unerringly through the night. Starshine gave him enough light to recognize the ground, and he circled to the left to avoid riding directly into a trap. He reined in above the ambush spot and sat his mount for interminable minutes, listening intently for unnatural sound. Once he thought he heard the clip of a hoof against a stone, but the sound was not repeated and he looked around slowly, probing the shadows.

When he was satisfied that he was alone he dismounted and tethered the horse to a low branch. He drew his pistol and moved slowly to a vantage point, then dropped to the ground and lay still, watching and listening. The silence was heavy, like an extra blanket on a warm night, and despite evidence to the contrary, Raven slowly accepted that there was someone out here, probably waiting for dawn. His instincts and experience prompted him to accept the fact, and he lay unmoving, his pistol ready, his patience inexhaustible.

An hour passed and the sound of a furtive foot cracking a twig in the undergrowth alerted him. He stiffened into full awareness and his lips pulled back against his teeth as he nodded. He was not surprised. His instincts never played him false. He waited, his breathing shallow, ears strained and picking up the other furtive sounds that reached him. Someone was trying to move silently through the brush, and coming in his direction.

Raven did not move a muscle. The sounds became louder as interminable moments passed. The darkness was impenetrable. There was a sharp breeze that rustled through the undergrowth and the branches of the trees along the stream. He breathed shallowly through his mouth, keyed up for action, and even when he heard the sound of the other man breathing he could not see anything. Then movement caught his keen gaze and a figure suddenly manifested itself directly in front of him.

He struck with the speed of a rattler, lashing out with his pistol. A dull thud sounded as the obdurate metal crashed against a Stetson. He struck again, and heard a groan from the man, who slumped into unconsciousness. Raven reached out and wrested a pistol from the stranger's hand.

Raven lay with a hand on his victim, looking around and listening for further unnatural sound. There was nothing, and now his instincts were at rest. He holstered his gun and felt in his pocket for a match. The tiny flare of light illuminated the face of the man he had struck, and he was surprised when he recognized the angular features of Clint Jackson. The deputy was beginning to stir, and Raven used Jackson's gun to cover the man as he groaned and began to show an interest in his surroundings.

'I got you covered, Jackson,' Raven said softly. 'Stay still and I won't kill you.'

'What in hell! How come you're lying out here like an animal, Raven?'

'What are you doing out here?' Raven countered.

'I was on my way to the ranch to see you.' Jackson spoke in an aggrieved tone.

'Yeah? Now tell the truth, will you? What were you doing skulking around here? Did you fire those shots at the house? Where's your horse? Why did you leave it to sneak in? Come clean or I'll bore you and leave you dead.'

'Hey, hold your horses. I never heard any shots. I'm here to take you back to town. I got a man there who knows Raven by sight and I want him to take a look at you. I was sneaking in to get the drop on you.'

'Why didn't you bring your witness with you? It would have saved time.'

'He's in the calaboose. Stig Ivey, an outlaw. I picked him up this afternoon. He says he knows Raven by sight.'

Raven felt a pang of emotion stab through his chest at the mention of Ivey. 'I doubt that. I never set eyes on Ivey. He disappeared without trace when I was looking for him.'

'Why were you looking for him?'

'To kill him.' Raven's teeth clicked together and he fell silent, his mind filled with bitterness while memories from the past flooded his thoughts.

'You can ride back to town with me,' Jackson said. 'Ivey will hang for what he's done. Mebbe you'd like to see him swing.'

'You ain't giving orders,' Raven said. 'In case you haven't noticed, I've got the drop on you. Let's go down to the ranch house where I can get some light on you. Don't try anything. I don't believe a word you've said. You're using the Raven question to cover your real intentions. Up on your feet. For the moment you better believe I'm Raven, so don't get any ideas about getting the better of me. Right now you're standing on the brink of hell, Jackson, and it won't take much to persuade me to send you over.'

'You're making the situation a lot worse for yourself.' Jackson spoke hoarsely as he scrambled to his feet. 'You can't take liberties with the law. I am a deputy, and manhandling me will make things worse for you.'

'I heard enough in town to know

you're mixed up in Beth Hallam's trouble, and I'll find out exactly where you stand before I'm done. Now get moving. We'll pick up your horse, then mine, and remember what I said about trying to get too clever.'

Jackson moved back up the slope and Raven followed him closely, Jackson's pistol cocked in his hand. Jackson's horse was waiting beyond the rim of the valley, and Raven made the deputy lead the animal while they walked through the darkness to where his own mount was waiting. The animal whickered softly as they neared it, and Raven tightened his girth and stepped up into the saddle. Jackson did the same and they rode to the trail that led into the valley.

The guard challenged them and Raven replied. They rode on to the house, and Mason called a challenge from the dense shadows flooding the porch. Jackson offered no resistance and they dismounted and entered the house. Mason followed them in, staring at the deputy with keen dislike in his gaze.

'He was snooping around out there?' Mason demanded. 'Hell, he draws pay from Monte Grand, and looks after that crook's interests around town. Pity you didn't kill him.'

'You got no call to talk thataway, Mason,' Jackson snarled. 'I've done you several favours around town.'

'You can do me a favour right now,' Raven interposed. 'Tell me why you were sneaking around out there.'

'I already told you, and I ain't changing my story because you wanta hear something different.' Jackson shook his head. His eyes were gleaming, his gaze filled with cunning as he considered his position. 'I'll do a deal with you, Raven. Let me go and I'll drop my efforts to prove your real identity.'

'You couldn't prove who I am if I drew pictures for you. Who knows you came out here?'

Jackson smiled. 'You don't think I'd

ride out without telling someone in town, huh? I got permission from Sheriff Wilson to chase this up. We need to know if a top gun has come into the county.'

'You'll get nowhere with him,' Mason cut in. 'Let me take him out and shoot him like the coyote he is. He's a bad smell around the county, and it'll ease our problems if we put him out of circulation. I know for a fact he draws pay from Monte Grand. You'll never get a better chance to cut the odds than this. A crooked lawman is bad news to everyone, and Jackson has got more twists than a rattlesmake.'

'What about Stig Ivey?' Raven demanded.

Jackson smiled. 'I guessed that name would stir you up. You've got a thing about that outlaw. What did he do to you?'

'All I know is that I'm gonna kill him when I lay eyes on him.' Raven spoke in an even tone. 'Is he in the town jail?'

'You'll have to ride in with me to find

out.' Jackson spoke casually but there was a tension in him that was noticeable.

'Don't trust him,' Mason said sharply. 'He's up to something, Drake. I wouldn't be surprised if he set the ambush that damn near killed Lorne Hallam. I reckon he's taken dough from Monte Grand. He's probably been paid to get rid of you.'

Raven smiled. 'Is that what this is all about, Jackson? If you are playing some deep game then you're gonna take a slug for your trouble. I'll ride into town with you, and if I find you are double-dealing, you'll be the first to collect a bullet.'

Jackson's face hardened and for a moment fear showed in his eyes. Then he nodded.

'It's like I told you,' he said. 'Stig Ivey is in jail, and I know that you, as Raven, would wanta see him through gunsmoke, so I'm giving you the chance.'

'What do you get out of it?' Mason

demanded. 'You never did a thing for nothing.'

'I want Ivey dead. If he is taken from my jail he'll never stand trial, and I want to see him done with. Raven is the only man who can put him down.'

'So Ivey has stepped on your toes, huh?' Mason demanded.

A door slammed somewhere in the house, and the next moment Beth appeared. Her expression hardened when she saw Jackson.

'What's he doing in my house? Get him out of here. He's not welcome on the spread, and he knows that.'

'We're trying to get to the bottom of why he is here,' Raven said. 'Mason, fetch Jackson's rifle from his saddle. I want to know if he's fired it recently.'

'I shot a coyote on my way here,' Jackson said as Mason departed.

Raven smiled. 'You've always got an answer, huh? But we'll pin you down before we're through.' He glanced at Beth, who was regarding Jackson as if he had crawled in under the door. 'I've got to ride into town with Jackson,' he told her. 'I'll be back some time tomorrow morning.'

'If Jackson's asked you to go with him then be careful. It will be a trick.' Beth dropped a hand to the gun she was wearing. 'I'm tempted to gutshoot him here and now. I know it will come to that before this business is settled. Jackson has been handling the situation for his own good. I could ask him many questions he wouldn't care to put answers to.'

'Such as?' Jackson's eyes glittered. 'You got it wrong, Beth. I'm just a simple deputy trying to do a tough job. I'm still trying to get a lead on who shot your father, and why.'

'Why do you want Pete in town? You must know by now that he isn't Raven.'

'I don't know any such thing, and there's a prisoner in the jail says he can identify Raven.'

'It'll be some kind of a trap,' Beth asserted. 'Don't trust him an inch.'

'He knows where he stands with me,'

Raven said curtly.

Mason returned with Jackson's rifle in his hand. 'It's been fired recently,' he said, thrusting the weapon under the deputy's nose.

'Never mind that now,' Raven cut in. 'Watch him, Mason. I need to talk to Beth before I leave.'

Beth frowned and led the way along a passage into an office. Raven gave her details about the shooting in which he had been involved earlier, and saw shock filter into her face.

'Floyd Buxton was planning to steal our steers?' She shook her head in disbelief.

'He was robbed blind, and thought Diamond Cross was responsible.' Raven was frowning. 'What do you want me to do about him?'

'I'll need to talk to him before any action can be considered,' Beth said gravely. 'If he has been robbed then he should be on our side. We'll set him straight and then see which way he jumps.'

'You're too trusting,' he told her.

'That's fine, coming from you. I wouldn't trust a snake or a coyote, but you're taking Jackson at his word. I didn't get you back from Mexico to set you up as a target.'

Raven smiled, his eyes glinting. 'I'll see you tomorrow,' he replied. 'Right now I got some work to do. Keep your head down around here until I get back.'

'It's Stig Ivey, isn't it? Jackson found the right bait to lure you. One mention of that outlaw's name and you forget everything else.'

Jackson sighed as he nodded.

'I guess that's about right. You hit the nail on the head.'

He turned on his heel and went back to Jackson. Mason was threatening the deputy with the rifle he was holding.

'Leave him be,' Raven said. 'We're riding out now. Take care of the place, Mason. Come on, Jackson. What are you waiting for? Let's ride.'

Jackson smiled and headed for the

door. Raven followed closely and they took to their saddles, riding across the yard and vanishing into the night. Raven rode on Jackson's right, content to let the deputy lead the way. The night was dark, the trail uncertain in the bad light. Jackson set a fast clip and their hoofs hammered the hard ground. Raven kept silent. His thoughts were centred upon the outlaw he had hunted in vain for a number of years, hoping that his luck was turning, aware that everything else would have to wait until he had paid the debt of blood he felt obliged to settle.

6

Raven wondered at Jackson's attitude as they rode through the night. The deputy remained obdurately silent during the long ride, and made no attempt to resist. He seemed quite happy to be returning to town as a prisoner. When Raven spotted the lights of Clayville in the distance it was he who broke the silence.

'It's time you told me what's behind your trip to the ranch, Jackson,' he said. 'What's waiting for me in town?'

'I told you. Stig Ivey is in jail, and I want you to kill him.'

'I don't buy that.' Raven shook his head. 'You're working for Grand, and Ivey was coming into the county to work for him, so why do you want Ivey dead?'

Jackson did not answer. Raven smiled.

'I don't work for Grand,' he persisted. 'You and Ivey are on the same side, so I reckon you're leading me into a trap. Grand wants me out of the way because I turned down an offer to work for him, so you've got to get rid of me, and you ain't man enough to do that by yourself.'

'I got one boss and that's Sheriff Wilson. I may appear to work for Grand, but it ain't so. We have to associate with law breakers in order to get at them.'

'So what's the talk about Stig Ivey being in jail? It isn't true, huh?'

'I was told to say that because it's well known that you are out to kill Ivey.'

'You mean Raven wants to kill Ivey. That ain't the same thing.'

'Forget about trying to bluff out your identity. Sheriff Wilson knows you by sight. He's aware that Beth sent for you, and why. If you are here to help Diamond Cross beat its trouble then you'll be tangling with the men the law wants, and Wilson reckons it would help if you worked with us instead of trying to fight a feud on your own. The sheriff is waiting in town to talk to you.'

'Why didn't you tell me this in the first place? You could have got yourself killed by sneaking up on me.'

'The sheriff didn't know which way you would jump. I heard Grand offer you a job. You could have gone for the highest stakes and worked against us.'

'So you and the sheriff are against Grand, huh?'

Jackson did not answer, and Raven lapsed into silence as they entered the rutted street. There were few lights burning at this time, and dense shadows surrounded them. Light and noise was coming from the saloon despite the lateness of the hour, and Raven felt his nerves tighten, keenly aware that he could be walking into a trap. There was dim light showing in the law office. Jackson rode to the hitching rail in front of the sidewalk and dismounted. Raven joined him, and stayed close to the deputy as they went into the office.

The big man seated at the desk in the office was wearing a sheriff's badge on his shirt front. He had been dozing until Jackson thrust open the door, and he stood up, blinking his dark eyes. He was heavily built, and looked tough. His fleshy face bore several small scars, as if he had at one time dived headfirst through a window. He was wearing a pistol low down on his right hip, and kept his hand well away from the weapon.

'Glad to see you, Raven,' he greeted, a crooked smile appearing on his thin lips. 'I didn't think you'd come.'

'I couldn't resist Jackson's offer.' Raven noticed that the sheriff was having difficulty speaking. 'What's going on, Sheriff. Lawmen don't wanta meet me unless it's with a gun in hand.'

'I know why you're in the county, and it looks like you're gonna do the job Beth wanted you for. That being the case, you and I are working towards the same end, so it makes sense for us to handle the chore together. I know there's a murder warrant out for your arrest, but it doesn't apply in Texas, unless someone has asked the Rangers to pick you up, so we could help each other. How does the proposition sound to you?'

'I can think of a dozen reasons why I should turn you down without a second thought, but if you're after the same thing I want then the idea of working with you catches me. The only way I would go along with it is for you to supply information and I'll do the shooting.'

'That's what I've got in mind.' Wilson pointed to a chair. 'Sit down and I'll give you a line on what's been going on around here. Clint, make some coffee.'

Raven sat down at the side of the desk while Jackson went through to a back room. Sheriff Wilson sat down on his padded chair and massaged his jaw.

'I've got some news for you,' Raven

said, and explained the incident involving Floyd Buxton's Rafter B outfit.

Wilson's face expressed shock, and he stirred uneasily in his seat.

'Jeez!' he exclaimed. 'You haven't wasted any time. I expected you to turn up and set this county alight, but you've done more in an hour than this department has accomplished in months. My hunch in getting you on my side looks good.'

'What about Buxton? Moran will be dead come morning. We couldn't move him, and a buckboard will pick him up tomorrow. He told me Buxton's plan. Rafter B was robbed so Buxton is getting his own back by robbing his neighbours.'

'I'll handle Buxton.' Wilson nodded. 'He ain't a factor in this set-up. Grand is the kingpin, the way I look at it, but he covers his tracks too well. I can't act until I've got proof, and that's where you come in. You can ferret around and get the deadwood on Grand.'

'Sounds all right from your point of

view,' Raven observed, 'but I'll be kneedeep in gunnies the minute I show my face on the street.'

Wilson smiled crookedly, then winced and lifted a hand to his jaw.

'That's the way it goes,' he said. 'But that's the reason you're here. You knew the score before you decided to throw in with the Hallams. Now you're in it up to your neck, and you can only go forward.'

'I can't argue with that.' Raven's thoughts were bitter as he nodded. 'I'll go along with you. Where do I start?'

'Show yourself in Lappard's saloon. That's all you'll have to do. Then take it as it comes.'

'It won't do for me to be seen coming in here,' Raven observed.

'You're right.' Wilson nodded. 'If I wanta get word to you I'll send Danny Delf. You know Danny — works in the livery barn. He's a good lad.'

'Sure. I'll get moving then.' Raven turned to the door and departed, then stepped back into the office again. 'One thing,' he said. 'Keep Jackson outa my way.'

'Consider it done.' Wilson tried to grin, and then pressed a hand quickly to his jaw.

Raven went out to the street and looked around. The town seemed desolate, hostile, and he swung into his saddle and rode along the street to the hitching rail in front of the saloon. His instincts were protesting at what he planned to do, but he had to find out if the sheriff was on the level, which meant following the first piece of advice the lawman had given him.

Dismounting, he eased his gun in its holster, thrust open the batwings, then stepped quickly into the saloon and took a swift pace to the right to place his back against the wall. He looked around. There were a handful of men present, and Raven could tell at a glance that most of them were gunnies — Grand's men, no doubt. He saw Kirk sitting at a table across the saloon, and two of the men with him were gun men who had been in the crowd in front of the office that morning.

All eyes swivelled towards Raven as he walked to the near end of the bar. The tender, polishing glasses, had frozen at the sight of him, his mouth gaping, and Raven took his manner as a warning. He was expected, and it was likely that a trap was waiting. He watched the long room bleakly. The piano player had lifted his hands from the instrument when the batwings opened, and now he got up from his seat and hurried out through a door in the back wall. Raven smiled and returned his hard gaze to the bartender.

'Close your mouth and gimme a beer,' he ordered, and the tender shook himself and hastened to obey.

A glass of foaming beer came sliding along the top of the bar and Raven picked it up with his left hand. He gulped half the contents of the tall glass, watching the room for movement as he did so. The silence in the saloon was overwhelming. A man turned away from the bar. He called a farewell to the bartender and went striding to the door, his steps hurried. The batwings swung behind him, the noise grating in the silence. Raven emptied his glass and set it down. The tender hurried forward.

'You want another?' he demanded nervously.

'No thanks.' Raven looked around the room again, his gaze fastening on Homer Kirk. The big man was grim-faced, his features showing apprehension. Raven grinned. 'Hey, Kirk, what orders did Grand give you today, huh? What have you gotta do about me?'

'I didn't get any orders about you,' Kirk replied. 'What are you talking about?'

The two gunmen stood up from Kirk's table and turned to face Raven. He knew by their expressions that they were primed to fight.

'We don't need orders,' one of them rasped.

'And we sure as hell ain't scared of you,' the other grated.

'Talk is cheap.' Raven stepped away from the bar, his right hand dropping to his side.

Both men went into a crouch, hands hovering above the butts of their holstered guns. Raven remained upright, waiting, composed and deadly. The silence in the saloon deepened. Kirk was frozen in his seat, both hands in plain view on the table. He was facing Raven across the room but his eyes were fixed on an imaginary spot on the batwings.

The gun man on the left was the first to break the tableau. His right hand flashed down to his holster and came up gripping his pistol, the movement triggering the second man into action, and he made a fast draw. Raven hardly seemed to move. His pistol appeared in his hand and exploded raucously, firing two shots so fast the reports blended into one roll of deafening sound. Both gun men took slugs. The one on the right managed to trigger his weapon but his muzzle was just clear of its holster and the bullet bored into the floor. The second man dropped his gun and followed it down to the floor-boards. The big room was shaken by the shots. Black gun smoke drifted. Glasses rattled on the back-bar, and then the echoes faded slowly.

Raven remained motionless, gun in hand. His keen gaze swept the saloon but no one else wanted trouble. He turned his attention to Kirk, who did not move a muscle.

'You got nothing to say, Kirk?' he demanded. 'Those two were in your pay.'

'I didn't tell them to take you on,' Kirk said thickly.

'Someone did. Who gave you orders to have Beth Hallam barred from the store?'

'That was an unfortunate mistake.' Kirk shook his head. 'It won't happen again.'

'You can bet your life it won't. I'm on

138

the Diamond Cross payroll now, and anyone with a complaint against the Hallams can step up and talk to me about it, likewise anyone wanting to cause trouble for the brand.'

Silence followed his words, and Raven was aware that his work here was finished. He holstered his gun and stepped to the batwings, wondering why the sheriff had sent him into the saloon. Wilson must have known a trap had been set for him and wanted the first shots in the war to be fired. He went out to the sidewalk and drew a long breath of the cool night air.

A gun flash split the dense shadows of an alley across the street. The bullet missed Raven by a scant inch because he reacted instinctively to the shot, throwing himself flat on the boardwalk as it rang out. He heard the solid thud of the slug striking the front of the saloon as he drew his gun, but he held his fire as a second gun blasted from a spot yards to the right. He saw a figure stagger forward from the alley and fall heavily in the street.

Raven frowned as he waited. Someone had bought into it on his side. He considered the possibilities. Was it the sheriff or Jackson? He shook his head, discounting both. Wilson had made it quite plain that he did not want to be associated with a notorious gunman. He peered around into the shadows, and heard retreating footsteps from the spot where he estimated the second man had been.

Full silence returned and Raven got to his feet. He crossed the street to where the sprawled figure was lying motionless and checked it. The man was dead, with a patch of blood spreading across his chest. Straightening, Raven looked around, his mind flitting over the incident. He wondered if Beth had followed him into town and had been watching his back. He could think of no one else who would step in on his side, but suspected that she would not have faded into the shadows if she had been responsible.

A man emerged from the saloon and stood with his back to the batwings, looking across the street at Raven.

'Come over here and take a look at this man,' Raven called.

The man started forward, then hesitated and turned to hurry away to the right. Raven shook his head. No one was keen to become involved. He crossed to his horse, swung into the saddle and rode back along the street to the law office. If Wilson or Jackson had shot the ambusher, he would still be out of the office. He trailed his reins and entered the office, to pull up short on the threshold. Both Wilson and Jackson were seated at the desk.

'We heard the shooting,' Wilson remarked. 'How did it go?'

Raven explained, and then said, 'What's going on? Are you two gonna sit around while I handle your dirty chores? Is that what you call working together?'

'We can't be seen to be in with you.' Wilson was frowning. 'Clint, go find out who has been killed and how the shooting is gonna be reported.'

Jackson arose and hurried out.

'Want some coffee?' Wilson offered.

'No thanks.' Raven explained about the ambusher along the street and mentioned the unknown gun that had intervened. 'I thought you had taken a hand.'

'Not us.' Wilson shook his head. 'Must have been someone with a grudge against Grand.'

'So what happens now? Have you got anyone else slated for killing?'

Wilson shook his head. 'You've cleared the town for us. Kirk and those three gunnies he had around him here were a big handicap.'

'What's to stop Kirk bringing in more gunnies? They're cheap.'

'He won't do that if you take him out to Diamond Cross. Hold him out there until I get further word to you. If Grand doesn't have Kirk as eyes and ears around here it'll ease matters considerable. Grand will think Kirk turned yellow when the gunnies were killed, and ran out, especially if you empty the safe in Kirk's office when you grab him. It will look like Kirk lined his pockets before splitting the breeze.'

Raven could see the wisdom in Wilson's thinking and turned to the door. He left quickly and led his horse along the street to Kirk's office. There was a light inside and Raven tried the door, which opened to his touch. He entered the outer office. The door leading to Kirk's office was ajar, and Raven heard sounds coming from within. He pushed the door open and peered in to see Kirk crouched beside the open safe, putting its contents into a leather bag.

'Leaving town?' Raven demanded, and Kirk sprang up as if he had been shot.

'What the hell!' he snapped. Sweat was dripping down his face and he cuffed it away with his left sleeve. 'I got business at Big G,' he added. 'What do you want?'

'You're invited to spend some time at Diamond Cross.' Raven smiled. 'Finish emptying the safe and we'll ride out.'

'I'm not going anywhere with you.' Kirk spoke harshly, but Raven thought the man sounded unsure of himself.

'You don't have a choice,' he advised. 'But there is an easy way and a hard way of doing it. How do you want it?'

'You're making a big mistake if you think you can put something over on Grand.'

'Let me worry about that. You make up your mind how you wanta go out to Diamond Cross.'

'I'll ride with you, if you put it like that, but under protest. I'd better leave this bag here.'

'No. Bring it along.'

Kirk finished emptying the contents of the safe into the bag and closed the heavy door. He locked the bag and stood up, turning towards Raven, his expression harsh. He was sweating, and a glimmer of fear showed in his eyes.

'What are you gonna do with me?' he demanded.

'Talk to you. What happens after that depends on how well you help me. I've got a big job on hand. I'm gonna fix everyone who is against Beth Hallam.'

'I can't tell you anything about that. You got the wrong man, Raven.'

'If I find you're telling the truth then I'll turn you loose,' Raven responded. 'Let's go.'

They left the office and Raven stayed close to Kirk, leading his horse while Kirk walked towards the stable. Kirk seemed eager now to leave town, and saddled a horse with the minimum of delay. Raven watched him closely but Kirk was not about to give him any trouble. They rode out across the back lots and headed towards Diamond Cross.

'Were you on your way to see Grand when I caught up with you?' Raven asked when they were clear of town.

'No. I was running out. I've had enough of the trouble around here. I can see which way the wind is blowing.'

'Running out with the contents of the safe, huh? How much cash have you got in that bag?'

'About ten thousand dollars. I reckon Grand owes me that much, the things I've done for him.'

'Tell me about it,' Raven urged.

'I'll do a deal with you. I'll give you the lowdown on what's been going on around here if you let me get the hell out before Grand learns what I'm doing.'

'You got a deal if what you can tell me is worth it,' Raven told him.

'How's this for a starter? Sheriff Wilson is bossing the rustling, and handles the crookedness going on around the county. He's in it with Grand. Between them they plan to clean up. Grand couldn't do it by himself, and he made an offer that Wilson couldn't resist. Grand is after Diamond Cross, but they're taking over the smaller ranches first. Buxton's Rafter B is next on their list. Wilson has already run off Buxton's cattle, and Buxton will be killed any time now. They'll probably get you to kill him now you're working with Wilson.'

'I'm working for Diamond Cross,' Raven cut in.

'Did Beth Hallam send you into town to kill my three gunnies?' Kirk countered.

'I didn't kill the one who was waiting on the street for me to leave the saloon.' Raven's thoughts were grim. It looked as if Wilson had played him for a sucker by using him to start the fight in the saloon.

'Jackson must have killed him,' Kirk said. 'Wilson is tidying up around town.'

'Who drygulched Lorne Hallam?'

'Jackson, probably. I heard Hallam was due to be hit. But someone slipped up. He wasn't killed. You're gonna lose out, Raven, despite who you are. You can't buck the odds against you. If you've got any sense you'll get out while you can. I've seen the writing on

147

the wall and I'm moving on.'

'I never quit on a job,' Raven said tersely. 'Push on faster, and keep talking. Fill me in on the details if you wanta walk clear of this. How does Wilson handle the rustling?'

'Grand's outfit out at Big G makes the steal. There are a dozen wideloopers out there ready to lift anyone's cows at the drop of a hat. Now what about it? Do I ride out of this? I've told you enough to get you started on your clean-up. I need to be a long ways from here come morning.'

'You'll be safe enough at Diamond Cross for a few days,' Raven decided. 'I need to check out what you've told me. There is one thing more. Where is Stig Ivey?'

'I heard you've been looking for Ivey. That's why Grand offered him rich pickings to show up here. He's gonna take care of you.'

'So that's how they plan to work it, huh? If I can get Ivey in my sights I'll thank Grand for it. Come on, let's make tracks. The sooner I get to work on this bad business the sooner everyone can relax.'

They pushed on at a canter, following the trail to Diamond Cross and, when they reached the valley where the ranch was situated, Raven pulled his horse to a slithering halt and peered down into the shadows surrounding the headquarters. A patch of fire was marring the unbroken darkness, and he could see figures running around in the uncertain gloom. The barn was ablaze, and even as his gaze registered the grim fact, Raven heard the distant sound of guns hammering and echoing.

7

'Stay with me, Kirk,' Raven ordered, and spurred his mount, forcing the horse into a gallop.

He rode swiftly into the valley, his eyes narrowed. Wilson had played it smart, he figured, getting him to clean up around town while Diamond Cross was attacked in the next stage of the crooked scheme that was unfolding. He glanced back over his shoulder to see Kirk coming along in his rear and faced his front, urging his horse to greater effort. The shooting around the ranch was dwindling away, and by the time he rode into the yard the attack had ended with nothing but fading gun echoes to mark its passing.

A harsh voice challenged from the shadows around the house and Raven replied with his name. Beth appeared on the porch, remonstrating loudly with

Mason as the gunman tried to keep her under cover.

'What have you been doing?' Beth demanded as she confronted Raven. 'I wanted you to stick around here. Look what's happened while you've been away. They've almost burned down the spread around us.'

Raven turned to look for Homer Kirk but there was no sign of him. Kirk had ducked out at the first opportunity.

'So what happened here?' Raven asked.

'Several guns opened up at the spread,' Mason reported. 'They shot holes into everything. All we could do was take cover until they stopped, and by that time the barn was burning.'

Several cowhands were fighting the fire with buckets of water drawn from the well in the yard. Raven thought they were wasting their time but said nothing. He considered what Kirk had told him and reached a decision.

'Mason, I want you to show me the way to Grand's Big G.'

'What, now?'

'Sure. I need to talk to Grand, and there's no time like the present.'

'It wouldn't be safe riding into his yard after dark.' Mason shook his head. 'Better wait until morning. How did you get on in town with Jackson?'

'You wouldn't believe it.' Raven took hold of Beth's arm and led her back into the house. 'I've warned you against leaving cover at night,' he reproved. 'I can't be in two places at once, and it looks like I got to ride herd on you until you get it into your head that it's dangerous out here.'

'Don't treat me like a child,' Beth protested. 'I can hold my own with any man. What did you do in town? Have they got Stig Ivey in jail?'

Raven explained what had occurred and Beth shook her head in disbelief as she gazed at him.

'Do you believe what Kirk told you?' she demanded. 'Could the sheriff be working on both sides of the law?'

'Kirk was stealing money from his

office when I walked in on him. He was set on making tracks, but fast. I reckon he gave me the rights of it. That's why I'm riding to Big G. I'll talk to Monte Grand and find out what's on his mind.'

'Are you serious about that?' Mason demanded. 'There must be better ways of getting us killed.'

'I only want you to show me to the place,' Raven told him. 'You'll come back here before I start any ruckus. Saddle up and wait for me. I'll be ready in a few minutes.'

Mason departed, shaking his head. Raven motioned for Beth to sit down, and joined her when she obeyed reluctantly.

'Any idea who was responsible for the shooting here?' he asked.

'They didn't give their names when they rode in,' she responded tartly.

'Tell me about your father. Apart from getting shot, did he have any other trouble around here? How long has the rustling been going on?'

'There's always trouble on any range, and this county has been no exception. But there's been nothing we couldn't handle.'

'Who caused the trouble? Floyd Buxton found a lot more than he could handle, and he's in deep now because of it.'

'We never found out who was doing it, and it died out before it really started. That was before this last business began. Someone has been stirring it up again. That's why I wanted you to come and help.'

'I'm trying to get a lead on who is behind it,' Raven said patiently. 'My hands are tied until something gives. Just point me in the direction of someone you can say with any certainty is responsible for what's been happening and I'll get on with the chore.'

'I think Monte Grand is responsible, and you've got some evidence that the law in town is crooked. I've always believed that about Clint Jackson, so what else do you want?'

'I can't go against the law without proof of their involvement. If I get it wrong, Wilson could put me behind bars and forget about me. I wouldn't be a lot of help to you then.'

A shot echoed across the yard and Raven ran out to the porch. He saw a rider at the gate, being covered by the guard. Mason was already running towards the gate, and Raven waited, gun in hand. He saw Mason grasp the bridle of the horse and come back towards the house, leading the rider.

'It's Homer Kirk,' Mason called. 'He's tied to his saddle.'

'What happened, Kirk?' Raven demanded.

'I was held up on the trail,' Kirk said raggedly. 'I couldn't see who it was. He was masked. He roped me to my saddle and brought me back here. He sent my horse towards the gate, and rode off the other way when the guard saw me.'

Raven shook his head. 'Someone took my part in town,' he observed. 'I was shot at by one of Kirk's gunnies, and before I could nail him someone did it for me. Now who do you suppose would do a thing like that?'

'What about Kirk?' Mason countered. 'What are we gonna do with him?'

'Keep him here until we can get around to him. You got somewhere safe to put him?'

'Sure.' Beth said. 'There's the store room. That will hold him. Put him in there, Mason, and lock the door.'

Mason untied Kirk and marched him away at gun point. Raven untied the leather bag Kirk had suspended from his saddle horn. He ushered Beth back into the house.

'If you've got a safe on the ranch then lock this bag in it,' Raven said. 'It holds the contents of Grand's safe in town. I'm riding out now, and I don't know when I'll be back.'

'I wish you wouldn't ride to Big G.' Beth's face betrayed worry as she gazed at him. 'Why don't you take some men to back you?'

'That's not the way to do it,' Raven said. 'I don't want to start a range war. I need to put an end to the trouble around here, not add to it.'

'Going to see Grand alone will get you killed,' she insisted. 'He knows who you really are and that you're working for me. You won't have a chance.'

'I have to find out what's in Grand's mind. I'll take Mason with me. He'll come back here as soon as I sight Big G.'

Beth shook her head. 'I know it's no use talking to you,' she said bitterly. 'I think seeing Grand is the last thing you should do. Why don't you go for Wilson and Jackson? You have Kirk's word that they are mixed up in our trouble.'

'I wouldn't take Kirk's word for anything.' Raven smiled. 'He was running out when I got to him, and not to be trusted. Stay on the ranch and keep your crew around the place until I get back.'

'You actually think you can ride into Big G and get away afterwards?' Beth sighed. 'There are some things even you can't handle, despite who you are.'

'You worry too much,' Raven observed. 'You got me up here from Mexico and threw this job into my lap. So why don't you let me get on with it? Remember what I've said about staying close to home.'

He turned on his heel and left the house. Mason was coming across the yard from the corral, riding his horse. The gun man reined in and gazed down at Raven.

'Fuller will hold Kirk in the bunk-house during the night. Are you sure you won't change your mind about riding to Big G?'

'Don't give me a hard time,' Raven said. 'I get enough of that from Beth. Let's hit the trail. I want you back here before morning.'

He swung into his saddle and they rode out. Mason set a fast clip through the night and Raven followed silently, permitting his thoughts full rein. He needed some hard evidence against the wrongdoers and, as far as he could tell, the easiest way of getting the deadwood on those wanting to bring down Diamond Cross was by confronting the man everyone reckoned was responsible for the situation. All the evidence pointed to Grand, but it was all circumstantial.

It was an hour before dawn when Mason reined up on a ridge and stepped down from his saddle. A strong breeze was blowing in Raven's face as he followed suit and stretched his legs. The dense shadows surrounding them permitted no vision. They were standing in unrelieved darkness.

'You can't see it but we're looking down on Big G,' Mason said quietly. 'It'll be getting light in thirty minutes. You want me to stick around until the sun shows?'

'No. I can handle it from here. Get back to Diamond Cross and make sure Kirk doesn't get away. I'll need him later.'

'Sure thing. Before you move in on

Grand, just remember that he runs a big outfit. There must be twenty riders on his payroll, and some of them are real salty.'

'Thanks for the warning.' Raven smiled. 'See you later.'

Mason turned away, swung back into his saddle and rode off. The sounds of his departure faded and full silence returned.

Raven squatted on the ground and waited for dawn to come. An indistinct greyness filtered into the blackness, and suddenly he began to pick out features that had been invisible to his keen eyes. He found himself looking down a long slope, and the outline of a single-storey building of adobe walls and a thick sod roof eventually took shape in the foreground, with a miscellany of smaller buildings dotted around in the background. Several horses were standing motionless in a small corral, and a larger stockade to the right, close to a bunkhouse, contained many more saddle horses.

Already smoke was issuing from the roof of the cook shack, and movement in front of the bunkhouse indicated that cowboys were beginning to prepare for the new day. Raven swung into his saddle and circled the ranch headquarters, aiming to fetch up behind the house. He stayed below the skyline on his approach, and finally kneehobbled his horse in a gully fifty yards behind the house and walked forward to the back wall of the building, where a rawhide door, stretched on a pole frame, would permit him unseen entrance.

The door opened to his touch and he entered a long, broad room. The pink adobe of its walls was relieved by natural trophies — a mounted antelope head, several Indian blankets, a rifle rack containing half a dozen long guns; rifles, carbines and shotguns, and there was a large painting of a herd of buffalo suspended above the wide fireplace. A big roll top desk stood beside a tall window overlooking the front yard, and

Monte Grand was seated at the desk on a leather armchair, his elbows on the desk and his chin in his hands.

Raven coughed politely and Grand straightened and turned his head, his right hand sliding inside his jacket to the bulge of a shoulder holster. When he recognized Raven, Grand brought his hand back into view and smiled.

'What took you so long?' he demanded. 'I expected you before this.'

'I've been kinda busy. I needed to check out some things before riding out this way.'

Grand frowned and shook his head. 'I hope you've got the rights of this business. I figured you were wrong when you turned down my offer of a job. Knowing your reputation, I had it worked out that you'd jump at the chance of earning big money.'

'You've got me wrong.' Raven smiled. 'I told you in town that I'd already taken a job with Diamond Cross, and I never go back on my word. Beth Hallam brought me back from Mexico and I'll stand by her, whatever happens. All I'm interested in is finding who is giving her trouble and putting a stop to him.'

'Even if it kills you?' Grand watched Raven's face like a snake watching a prairie dog.

'That's right.' Raven could feel a chill sensation spreading through his nervous system, aware that his instincts were warning of imminent trouble. He tried to dispel the sensation but it persisted, and he had experienced it many times in the past. It always came to him when he was facing impending action.

'I felt sure you'd come to tell me you'd changed your mind about my offer of a job, that you would accept it.' Grand straightened his massive shoulders and moved back to his desk. He motioned Raven to a nearby seat and dropped carelessly on to his leather chair. 'If you haven't come to take a job with me then why are you here?'

'I need information. I heard that

you've hired an outlaw to take care of me in the event I don't join your payroll, namely Stig Ivey. I've wanted to kill Ivey for a long time.'

'I heard how Ivey's last bank raid turned out. The way it is told, your mother and brother were killed in the crossfire. Ivey never robbed another bank after that.'

'He dropped out of sight or I would have caught up with him and killed him. Is he coming here?'

Grand shook his head. 'I wouldn't hire a criminal like Ivey to handle any business of mine. I have a good crew to take care of the trouble that's coming. I wanted you because I'm short of a gun boss, and I've heard enough about your reputation to know that you are the best.'

'You're talking as if you're not responsible for the trouble facing Diamond Cross. Do you have plans for taking over the Hallam spread?'

Grand shook his head again. 'Not guilty. I've heard the talk and it doesn't bother me. I can live with it. I can work to find the real culprit while folks are blaming me. You can rest assured that I have no designs on the Hallam spread, or anything else around here that I cannot buy.'

'You're not responsible for the rustling that's been going on? Didn't you bring in a bunch of wideloopers to steal the range blind?'

'I heard what happened to Floyd Buxton, and I can tell you that my crew was not responsible. They trailed the stolen Rafter B herd into the badlands, where the tracks petered out. The report I got stated that Diamond Cross was responsible for the steal. Have you talked with Ham Sheridan?'

Raven shook his head. 'He quit cold the instant I walked on to the ranch. The rustling of the Rafter B herd was made to look like the work of Diamond Cross, and Buxton took the bait. He planned to steal from Diamond Cross to even the score. That won't happen now. I think I got you dead to rights,

Grand, and as soon as I can prove it I'll pay you another visit.'

'When you get proof on that rustling you'll realize that I am not responsible.'

'You sound too sure of yourself. If you believe what you're telling me then someone is feeding you false information. Who handles that side of your business?'

'Homer Kirk.'

'Well, that figures!' Raven laughed.

Grand's face changed expression. A chill light appeared briefly in his eyes and his whole manner took on raw unfriendliness.

'What do you know that I don't?' he demanded.

'Homer Kirk has lit out for other parts, and he cleaned out your safe before he left town last night.'

'What caused him to run?'

'There was a set-up in town for my benefit.' Raven explained about riding in with Clint Jackson and how the sheriff had asked him to work along with the law. 'When I'd killed the gunnies protecting Kirk in town, he upped stakes and left.'

'Do you know where he went?'

'I caught him and took him out to Diamond Cross because I thought I could use him, but he got away when we rode into an attack being made on the ranch.'

'What attack, and by whom?' Grand was apparently unaware of the incidents Raven described.

'I don't know yet. It wasn't much. The barn was fired. I reckon it was Buxton's work.'

'So you don't know where Kirk is right now?'

'No.' Raven's face was expressionless as he lied. 'He's your problem, not mine.'

'Something is wrong.' Grand was frowning. 'You'd better keep an open mind on this business until you get something to back up your suspicions. What do you make of the sheriff and his deputy? Don't they have some questions to answer?'

'I'll get around to them in due course, but I'm working at a disadvantage. My reputation is a big handicap. If I put a foot wrong I'll wind up behind bars, where I can't help anyone.'

'So why did you turn down the advantage of working for a big outfit? No one would touch you if you rode for Big G.'

'I'll think about that over the next day or so. It won't take me long to stick the blame where it belongs. I expect to see you again.'

'Any time,' Grand replied.

Raven went to the back door and departed. He walked away from the house to the spot where his horse was waiting, wondering why his visit here had gone so smoothly. He had expected to walk in with no trouble, and then have to fight his way out. But nothing happened as he mounted and rode away. He saw two riders appear around the front corner of the house. They saw him but ignored him, and he rode steadily until he was in the clear, his right hand close to the butt of his holstered gun.

He turned for Diamond Cross, and had covered roughly two miles when he got a feeling that he was being followed. He did not turn in the saddle, and gave no indication of what he suspected, but as he continued, the feeling grew stronger, and he began to anticipate a bullet in the back.

He crossed a ridge, slid from the saddle, and crawled back to the skyline to search for whoever was trailing him. He saw nothing, and looked left and right, aware that someone was by-passing his position. He caught a flicker of movement off to the right and spotted a rider disappearing behind a ridge. He moved back to his horse and began to trail the unknown rider.

When he finally got a look at the rider he was surprised to recognize Ham Sheridan, and followed the ex-Diamond Cross ramrod, wondering why the man had quit his job so precipitately. Sheridan seemed to be heading for a definite destination, not riding casually, and Raven had his work cut out to remain unseen. He eased off to one side and took advantage of the undulations of the range to avoid being spotted. Sheridan's head was constantly on the move, checking out his surroundings as if he expected trouble.

It soon became clear to Raven that Sheridan was heading for Diamond Cross, and it seemed the ex-ramrod had been snooping around Big G. Wondering about the apparent mystery, Raven was content to follow and watch. The greater part of the job in hand was watching and studying points, and he needed to find many answers before he resorted to action.

It was well after noon when Sheridan rode behind the ranch house at Diamond Cross, and Raven watched the big man sneak to the back door. The sun was burning in a cloudless sky and heat lay packed against the baked ground. Raven was sweating as he left his horse in cover and followed

Sheridan to the house. The ex-ramrod opened the kitchen door and disappeared inside the building. Raven followed moments later, gun in hand.

The drone of voices was coming from a room on the right in the passage leading through to the front of the house. Raven approached the half open door and pushed it wide with his left toe. His gun was levelled, and he paused when he saw Beth seated at a table with Sheridan standing before her. Beth caught the movement of the door opening silently and glanced past Sheridan, who turned swiftly, his hand leaping to the butt of his holstered pistol.

'Don't even think about it,' Raven said. 'What's going on?'

Sheridan looked sheepish. He lifted his hand clear of his waist, shaking his head. Beth sprang to her feet and hurried around the table to stand in front of Sheridan, shielding him with her body.

'Ham is still working for me,' she

gasped. 'Put your gun away, Pete.'

Raven gazed at the girl's pale face as he holstered his gun slowly. At that moment a gun blasted somewhere at the front of the house and harsh echoes fled through the heavy silence. Raven backed out of the room, turned, and ran towards the sound of the shot as more shooting erupted. Someone was forcing the issue.

8

Gun smoke was drifting across the yard when Raven paused on the porch to look around, and his quick gaze took in several puffs of black smoke along the line of the stream. Several men were shooting at the house. Raven slid back into cover when a slug hammered into the front wall. He lifted his Colt as Sheridan appeared at his side.

'It'll be Buxton and some of the rustlers, I expect,' Sheridan said. 'Let me take a look.'

He pushed his big frame into the doorway. Raven grasped his shoulder and pulled him back into cover when a bullet plunked into the woodwork beside his head. But Sheridan eased forward again, gazing intently across at the stream.

'Well?' Raven demanded. 'Do you recognize anyone?'

'Yeah.' Sheridan moved back into cover, his expression registering surprise. 'Clint Jackson is out there, and it looks like he's got a posse with him.'

'Jackson!' Raven felt a stab of shock. 'What's he doing, shooting up the spread?'

'Want me to go out and ask him?' Sheridan grinned. 'I thought you were well in with the local law.'

'So did I. But I'll get back to Jackson later. You're the one that interests me at the moment. I trailed you from Big G. What were you doing out there?'

'Watching your back. I was following you yesterday, and nailed that gunnie who was laying for you when you left the saloon last night.'

Raven frowned. 'You've been playing a mighty dangerous game.'

'Someone's got to take chances. Beth suggested it before you showed up. I've got my own ideas about who's behind our trouble, and I pretended to walk out so I could look around and try to get a pointer on the rustlers. I foiled Buxton's attempt to rustle our stock before I went to town, and lucky for you I was on hand when you rode in to talk to Wilson. You made a bad move there. Wilson used you to get rid of Kirk's gunnies, and I reckon Jackson is here now to arrest you for shooting those galoots. The local lawmen are crooked, and you're gonna have to handle them before you go any further.'

'And I suppose it was you who caught Kirk when he got away from me last night!'

'Yep. He thought he'd got clear, and he sure didn't appreciate being brought back. Are you still holding him?'

'As far as I know. What about Monte Grand? I heard the talk that he's behind all this crookedness, but when I spoke to him this morning he gave me a different impression.'

'I've got nothing against Grand yet.' Sheridan shook his head. 'Like I said, it's got to be Wilson and Jackson providing the muscle for the stealing that's going on, and matters won't ease until they're put out of business. They're handling the rustling, but I reckon someone else is plotting to take over Diamond Cross, and we need to find out who is back of that before we come down on Wilson and Jackson.'

'Are you sure it ain't Grand?

Sheridan shook his head. 'I ain't sure of anything where Grand is concerned, but we can get around to him later. Right now we better stop Jackson from shooting up the place.'

Raven narrowed his eyes as he peered across the valley. Occasional shots were being fired at the ranch from three different positions along the stream, which were marked by puffs of drifting smoke. He nodded.

'Keep them busy from here,' he decided. 'I'll get the drop on Jackson.'

He turned instantly, and almost blundered into Beth, who was standing silently behind him. She followed him to the back door.

'I heard what you and Ham were

saying,' she said. 'I'm sorry I deceived you about Ham. We both thought it was a good idea.'

'It could have got Sheridan killed. But he saved me in town so I guess he was doing the right thing. Stay under cover until I get back. I'm gonna pick up Jackson.'

He left the house and went to the spot where his horse was waiting. Expecting to find one of Jackson's men watching the animal, he circled the spot and moved in from the far side. He saw Jackson crouching in the brush in ambush with a rifle in his hands, and sneaked in close, his pistol ready. The big deputy jumped when Raven spoke to him.

'Drop that rifle and get your hands up,' Raven ordered. 'It's time we had a serious talk, Jackson.'

The big deputy dropped his rifle as if it had suddenly become too hot to hold. He stood up quickly, lifting his hands away from the pistol holstered on his right hip. His face was showing surprise, and fear glimmered in his eyes.

'I never heard you moving in on me,' he complained hoarsely.

'So why are you shooting up the place? I thought you, the sheriff and me are pards now. What's gone wrong with our deal?'

'Wilson sent me to tell you Stig Ivey and his gang showed up in town during the night. Ivey is looking for you.'

Raven gazed grimly at the deputy. He saw Jackson swallow nervously.

'So why wait for me with a rifle instead of riding in normally?' he queried.

'Wilson wants me to take you in. It's got to do with the shooting of Kirk's gunnies last night. A couple of witnesses came forward to say they saw you draw first. They're swearing to the fact that you didn't give the gunnies a chance. We're talking about a murder charge, and the sheriff says he's got to go through the motions of arresting you to keep everything under control.'

'So why didn't you ride up to the house to arrest me?' Raven persisted.

Jackson shrugged. 'I'm only obeying orders. Wilson wanted the posse to toss a few slugs into the ranch to make your arrest look good. He's sure the men causing the trouble in the county are riding for Diamond Cross. It's all part of a big cover up until we can get the deadwood on the boss of the crooked deal.'

'I never heard such trash.' Raven motioned with his pistol. 'Lead the way into the house. We'll get down to grass roots before we go any further. I'm not happy with you, Jackson. You wouldn't know the truth if it came up and hit you on the chin.'

'I'm only telling you what Wilson said I should say,' Jackson protested. 'I don't know what the hell is going on.'

'You and me both!' Raven took the deputy's pistol from its holster and followed him into the house. Jackson saw Sheridan talking to Beth and his expression changed. Raven noticed

Jackson's surprise and mentioned it.

'I heard that Sheridan skipped out when you arrived,' Jackson shrugged. 'So what's he doing here? Looks like someone is running a sandy on the law.'

'Never mind.' Raven gave Jackson's explanation for his actions.

Sheridan cursed mildly and moved in menacingly on the big deputy, cocking his right fist.

'Let me take him outside,' he suggested. 'I'll get the truth out of him.'

'No.' Raven unloaded Jackson's pistol and thrust the weapon into the deputy's hand. 'Cover me with that when we get on the porch, and then call the posse in. Sheridan, tell your crew to hold their fire, and keep Jackson under your gun. If he looks like trying his own thing then shoot him, lawman or not. I got the feeling we're wasting time. We've got to get something moving, and fast.'

'Sure.' Sheridan grinned and pulled his gun. 'Play it straight, Jackson, or you're dead.'

They went out to the porch and

Jackson stuck the muzzle of his pistol against Raven's spine. A bullet smacked into the yard a dozen feet in front of the porch as if to question the situation, and Jackson waved the come-on signal to his men across the stream. Sheridan shouted to his crew to hold their fire. They waited tensely, and minutes later four riders appeared beyond the gate and rode warily into the yard.

'Know any of them, Sheridan?' Raven demanded.

'Nope. They're all strangers to me.'

Raven stepped backwards until he was standing beside Jackson, who did not move, apart from letting his gun hand drop to his side. Raven took the empty weapon from the deputy and stuck it into his belt. The riders came up to the porch and reined in.

'What's going on, Jackson?' one of them demanded.

'There's a change of plan,' Raven said, and drew his gun. 'Hands up and sit still while we draw your fangs.'

The four men were disarmed, and

Raven turned to Mason, who was coming forward leading several of the Diamond Cross crew.

'Do you still have Kirk under guard?' Raven asked.

'Sure.' Mason grinned. 'He's in the store room back of the house, and there's a guard on the door.'

'Fetch Kirk out when you put these men inside, and bring him into the house,' Raven directed.

'Do you want Jackson locked in?' Mason demanded.

'Yeah. He's playing a strange game. We'll hold him until we know what's going on.'

The prisoners were led away. Raven went back into the house, followed by Sheridan, and Beth came to him, her expression showing unease.

'What happens now?' she demanded, clasping her hands together.

'I don't know.' Raven shook his head. 'If I had a line on what's going on I'd go for the rustlers, or whoever, and put them out of it. But these men against you are dug in too deep to unearth. The only men I've got a line on are the sheriff and Jackson, and they're law men. I can't shoot them up without proof or I'll be outlawed for sure, and then we'd all lose. We need to know who is behind the deep game, and who drygulched your father. Then we'd have an idea which direction we need to take. But, as it is, I don't know which way to turn for the best. If I make a wrong move I'll only add to your trouble.'

'While I was in town after I left here the day you turned up, I kept my ear to the ground,' Sheridan said. 'I hoped to get a slant on the trouble through loose talk, but I didn't hear a thing that would help, and that says a lot about this crooked business. From the little I do know I think we should go for Sheriff Wilson, bring him out here, and sweat the truth out of him. With both Wilson and Jackson out of it we'll cut off the hands of the crooked outfit, and mebbe the truth will come out.'

Raven nodded. 'I was thinking along those lines myself,' he mused. 'Let's hear what Kirk has to say before we decide what's next.'

'I'm against taking action against the law,' Beth said worriedly.

'I don't see any other way,' Raven replied. 'But don't worry about it. I'll find the weak link in their chain.'

Kirk entered the house with Mason at his back. He looked around uncertainly, and Raven motioned to a chair.

'Sit down, Kirk. You got one last chance to get out of this mess.'

Kirk sat down on the edge of the seat. He glowered at Sheridan, who drew his pistol and went through the motions of checking the weapon. The silence in the big room was heavy, and tension filtered into the atmosphere. Raven allowed the silence to go on for some moments, until Kirk swallowed nervously.

'What do you want from me?' Kirk demanded at length.

'Why were you running out on

Monte Grand?' Raven asked.

Kirk shrugged. 'Personal reasons. I don't want to talk about them.'

'You don't have to talk about anything,' Raven smiled. 'But if you clam up you won't be going anywhere until this business has been sorted out. Then it'll be too late. So tell me what spooked you into making a run for it.'

'I got tired of taking the orders I was getting. I was forced to act tough around town, and that didn't sit too well with me.'

'You had three gunnies to back you,' Raven observed, 'and you seemed to enjoy getting tough with Beth when I walked into your office.'

'You can say that again,' Beth interposed.

'Why were you putting pressure on Beth?' Raven persisted. 'Did Grand give you an order to do so?'

'Yeah. He wanted Diamond Cross to stop using the town.'

'Why?'

'He never said. I got my orders, and had to carry them out. While I did what I was told there would be no come-back. But I could see the way things were turning, and decided to get out before I became too involved. When you killed my three men I figured I would be next. I knew the sheriff sent you in to do his dirty work, and Wilson wanted me out of the way.'

'You're talking but you're not saying anything,' Raven said sharply. 'I want the deadwood on what is happening around here. Give me some details of crimes committed and who carried them out.'

'I don't know anything about that. I just did my job with no questions asked.'

'You don't know who drygulched Beth's father?'

'No. I never even heard talk about that.'

Raven felt impatience rising inside. 'Where's the bag Kirk had on him? I saw him putting the contents of his office safe in that bag. Mebbe we can find something from that.'

Beth left them to enter the ranch office. She returned a few moments later carrying the leather bag Kirk had carried. Raven opened it and turned out the contents on a table. There were wads of paper money and a stack of papers.

'You won't find anything but business documents there,' Kirk said.

Raven scanned through the papers, and found they were mainly accounts of the various businesses Monte Grand owned in town. Kirk evidently handled business affairs meticulously. There was nothing that was illegal.

'I told you there was nothing wrong in there,' Kirk said when Raven turned away from the table. 'I didn't do a damn thing that was against the law.'

'All this money,' Raven observed. 'Why wasn't it paid into the bank?'

For a moment, Kirk looked uncertain, and Raven noted the fact.

'Monte doesn't have an account at

the bank. He takes care of his own cash.'

'So Grand's business cash lies around in the office in town, huh?' Raven queried.

'There was always a gunman in the office. Grand thought it was safer that way.'

Raven's patience became exhausted. He motioned to Mason.

'Put him back in that store room. If he does know anything, he ain't gonna tell us. I'll go into town and talk to the sheriff. We know he's up to something, and although I don't like the idea of confronting him I don't have a choice. I'll drop on to him when he's not expecting it, and see what he's got to say under pressure.'

Kirk was taken out. Raven paced the big room for some moments, thinking over his options. Beth and Sheridan watched him in silence. Beth was worried, and it showed in her face. When Raven ceased his pacing, the girl touched his arm.

'You'll need to eat before riding into town. I'll get something for you. Will you take Mason along?'

'No. I ride alone. I'll eat before I leave. I won't want to be in town before sundown.' Raven looked at Sheridan. 'You'll hold the fort here, huh? Be ready for anything. Don't let anyone leave the place before I return.'

Sheridan nodded and departed. Raven followed Beth into the kitchen and watched her preparing a meal. The sun was at its zenith. He had to waste away the afternoon before he could get into town unseen. When the meal was ready he sat down to eat, and had barely started when a rider pounded into the yard. He pushed back his chair and arose, but paused when a woman's voice called out on the porch.

'Beth, it's me, Sarah Jane.'

'Sit down and eat,' Beth said, and Raven dropped back into his chair. 'I'll talk to Sarah Jane on the porch until you've finished.'

'Find out from her what's been

happening in town,' he replied. 'She might know something.'

Beth departed and Raven ate his meal. He was mopping up gravy with a piece of bread when Beth returned to the kitchen, followed by Sarah Jane. The girl greeted Raven cheerfully.

'Sarah Jane has a lot of news,' Beth said, 'and I think you should hear some of it. Sit down, Sarah Jane, and I'll make coffee.'

Raven studied the girl's face as she sat down across the table from him. She seemed worried, and excitement laced her voice when she spoke.

'I've seen Stig Ivey,' Sarah Jane said. 'He's walking around town as if he owns the place, and there are four hard cases with him. The sheriff is on friendly terms with Ivey, and I don't understand that because everyone knows Ivey is an outlaw with a price on his head.'

Raven clenched his hands. 'Thanks for telling me,' he said. 'That's worth knowing.'

'The town has practically closed

down,' Sarah Jane continued. 'Everyone is afraid of the outlaws. They've taken over the saloon and are making a lot of noise in there. I heard that Ivey is waiting for you to get word of his arrival. He expects you to turn up there for a showdown.'

'Who's paying him to get rid of me?' Raven mused. 'Someone's brought him in as an answer to me coming here on your side, Beth.'

'My father has closed the bank,' Sarah Jane said. 'He wanted me out of the way so he suggested I come out here to see you, Beth. He told me to stay with you for a few days.'

'Usually he's keen for you to stay away from me,' Beth observed.

'Only because he's afraid of the trouble you're in. Can I stay?'

'Sure.' Beth nodded. 'I'll be glad of your company.'

Raven arose. 'I'd better be making tracks. I can't waste any more time.'

'Take some men with you,' Beth suggested.

'No. I'll handle this myself.' Raven smiled. 'I've got a feeling that your problems will soon be over, Beth.'

He departed quickly, and found Sheridan waiting on the porch.

'Sarah Jane told me about Ivey and his gang being in town,' Sheridan said. 'I'd like to ride in with you.'

Raven shook his head. 'No. You've got to keep the ranch safe. Be ready for anything. I'll see you later.'

He swung into his saddle and rode out of the yard, looking back once to see Beth and Sarah Jane standing on the porch. Beth was talking animatedly to Sheridan. Raven faced his front and sent his black into an easy lope. His face stiffened into an expressionless mask, but emotion was rampant in his breast. At the moment he could think of nothing but facing Stig Ivey through gun smoke.

9

It was late afternoon when Raven sighted Clayville. He reined into cover just outside the town and hobbled his horse in dense brush. It was too light for him to ride in openly and he did not like leaving the horse too far away in case he needed to make a fast getaway, but impatience was spurring him and he needed to get to grips with the unknown men causing trouble for Diamond Cross. He crossed the open space to the back lots on the left-hand side of the wide street and lost himself in a maze of shanty dwellings, angling towards the street until he was at the rear of the jail. He eased into the doorway of a barn to look around.

His thoughts were running fast. His whole life had been geared to confronting and killing Stig Ivey. For several years he had hunted the outlaw unsuccessfully. Now Ivey was here in town, apparently waiting for him to arrive, but he had Diamond Cross trouble to handle. He experienced a mental struggle between the two courses facing him, and finally decided that he could always come back to the trouble in this county, but Stig Ivey might not wait so he had to deal with his personal problems at once.

He went along the back lots to the saloon and entered by the rear door, palming his Colt as he made his way to the bar, where he stood in a doorway looking around for Ivey. There were only two men in the saloon, and one of them was the bartender.

Raven went forward, and both men froze when they saw him. The bartender stepped back quickly from the bar, hands in plain view, his face expressing disquiet.

'You look like you've seen a ghost,' Raven observed.

'You're too late,' the bartender replied. 'Ivey and his gang rode out half an hour ago. They were in here about two hours, waiting for you to show up. Ivey was getting impatient towards the end, and I heard him say as he left that they'd have to come back for you.'

'Any idea where he went?' Raven asked impassively.

'He didn't confide in me.' The bartender shook his head.

Raven departed by the back door and hurried back to the rear of the law office. He had the feeling that some deep plan was unfolding around him because he was unaware of the identity of the men running the crooked business. But all that was about to change, he vowed.

He moved into the alley to the right of the jail and walked along it to the street. Peering from the alley-mouth, he found the street practically deserted, but that did not surprise him.

The street door of the law office was open, and a man was sitting on a chair on the sidewalk in front of the doorway. Raven frowned. As far as he knew, the law department consisted of Wilson and Jackson, but the lounging man was wearing a deputy badge. Raven stepped out of the alley and walked to the deputy. The chair had been placed right in front of the doorway and the deputy's sprawled legs blocked the sidewalk. The man was asleep, snoring softly.

Raven kicked the deputy's left boot. The man snorted and started up. His face, covered with short, black stubble, said much about him. His dark eyes were bleary, as if he had been drinking heavily. He gazed belligerently at Raven and his right hand dropped to the gun holstered on his hip although he made no attempt to draw it.

'What the hell do you want?' he demanded. 'Didn't you see I was asleep?'

'Where's the sheriff?'

'Inside. Where do you expect him to be?'

'You're blocking the doorway. Move your chair to one side.'

The deputy cursed mildly and lurched to his feet. He smelled of whiskey, and almost fell to the sidewalk. Recovering his balance, he moved the chair to one side, dropped on to it, and was sleeping again before Raven could step into the office.

Raven crossed the threshold and peered around the dim interior. Sheriff Wilson was sitting at the desk, his chin in his hands. He was asleep, snoring heavily. Raven shook his head. A gang of outlaws had been in town and the local law department was asleep, or pretending to be. He closed the door quietly and eased home the heavy bolt on the inside. A floorboard creaked as he walked to the desk, and Wilson opened his eyes immediately, instinctively reaching for his holstered gun.

'That's not a good idea,' Raven said sharply and Wilson froze in his seat.

'What's eating you?' the sheriff demanded. 'I thought we were working together.'

'That's what I thought, until Jackson

turned up at Diamond Cross with a posse and began to shoot up the place. When I caught him he said he was acting on your orders.'

'I never gave him any such orders. That damn fool never gets anything right. It's about time I fired him. I sent him out to Diamond Cross to warn you that Stig Ivey and some of his gang are in town. Ivey wants to meet up with you.'

'He'll do that soon enough. How come he's wandering around town while I got a gun reception laid on when I arrived, and I ain't even wanted by the law?'

'Local politics, I guess.' Beads of sweat had broken out on Wilson's forehead. 'It looks like someone around here didn't want you operating in the county.'

'And who would that be?'

Wilson shrugged. He had spread his fingers on the top of the desk, palms down, and was pressing hard, his knuckles showing white.

'You better get rid of your gun,' Raven suggested. 'Use your finger and thumb, lift it out of the holster slowly, and put it on the desk.'

He waited until Wilson had complied. The sheriff pushed the weapon to the far corner of the desk, as if removing temptation. He seemed easier when he leaned back in his chair.

'So you've got a couple of witnesses to the shooting in the saloon who are saying I didn't give those men I killed a fair chance. Jackson said you wanted me to come back to town with him so you could put me behind bars — just for the sake of appearances.'

'I don't know anything about that.' Wilson shook his head. 'I didn't tell Jackson anything of the sort.'

'So Jackson is working to a plan of his own, huh?' Raven leaned his hands on the desk and thrust his face towards the sheriff. 'I reckon the two of us should ride out to Diamond Cross and talk to Jackson. That way we might get at the truth.'

'I can't leave town right now, not with Stig Ivey on the loose.' Wilson shook his head.

'What are you gonna do about that outlaw? How are you gonna take him?'

'I ain't gonna try. He won't bother honest folk around here. He'll make tracks when he's killed you.'

'Who brought him into the county?'

'I don't know. He wouldn't tell me when I asked. It's obviously someone who doesn't want you around.'

'You're a liar, Sheriff!' Raven's voice was quiet.

Wilson flinched. 'You got no call to talk to me like that,' he complained. 'I've bent over backwards to keep in with you.'

'Sure. You even let me kill Kirk's gunnies for you. Now you're hoping I'll go up against Ivey and his gang and die in the attempt. I'd sure like to know what's in that quicksand you call a mind. Maybe we should clear the air a little, huh? Get on your feet, stick your gun back in your holster, and we'll try conclusions.'

Wilson's lined face took on an expression of concern as he shook his head and settled himself deeper in his seat.

'That ain't a contest,' he said sharply. 'I won't lift a gun against you.'

Raven drew his gun so fast the movement was blurred by its speed. Wilson jerked back in his seat at the sudden appearance of the weapon, and reared up in fright. A smile touched Raven's lips as he leaned across the desk and pressed the muzzle of his weapon against the sheriff's forehead.

'Have you been this close to death before, Sheriff? My gun is hair-triggered. You take a deep breath and it's likely to trip.'

'You ain't scaring me, Raven. I know you ain't ever murdered a man in your life. I'm quite safe so long as I don't make the mistake of reaching for a gun, and you ain't likely to make a start on the murder trail by shooting a sheriff in cold blood. You're running around in circles, like a dog on a chain, and you ain't getting any closer to the right answers. You came into town yesterday and I got you to remove Kirk's gunnies for me. You've come back again now, looking for someone to shoot. You were expected to tangle with the Ivey gang here, but they had to ride out half an hour ago, and while you're away from Diamond Cross the ranch will be taken over by those men who are running the crooked deal.'

Raven gazed into the sheriff's narrowed eyes. Wilson was sweating badly now, filled with uneasiness, as if he were afraid of Raven's reactions to his words.

'It ain't any of my doing, Raven,' he said. 'I take orders like everyone else.'

'Who is giving the orders?' Raven demanded.

Wilson shook his head. 'Shouldn't you be riding back to Diamond Cross?' he countered. 'Something bad is gonna happen to Beth and her father. It's the only way the ranch can be taken over.'

'You're right, and I'm taking you

with me. Get up. Make for the back door. Where do you stable your horse?'

'The barn out back, and it's ready-saddled. I've been waiting for you. What took you so long?'

Wilson got to his feet, smiling tensely now. He picked up the cell keys and hurried into the cell block with Raven close behind, but he was suddenly nervous. He had trouble unlocking the back door, and Raven jabbed him with the muzzle of his pistol.

'If you're trying to set me up you'll be making the biggest mistake of your life,' Raven warned. 'There's one thing I hate more than Stig Ivey and that's a crooked sheriff. You're gonna be hard put to survive this fight, Wilson, and that's if you help me every way you can. So try to trick me again and you'll be on Boot Hill tomorrow, with six feet of dirt piled on your chest.'

Wilson paused in his fumbling to open the door. He turned to look at Raven, his face beaded with sweat.

'On second thoughts, you better not

go out this way,' he said hoarsely.

'So you have got something planned, huh?' Raven smiled. 'Open the door.'

Wilson made a big job of unlocking the door. When he had opened it he backed away, determined not to leave by it. Raven grasped him by a shoulder and thrust him forward.

'You lead the way,' Raven snapped.

Wilson opened the door wide but still edged away. Raven thrust him heavily in the back. Wilson staggered outside, turned quickly and tried to get back in cover. A gun blasted from the back lots. Wilson cried out and jerked under the impact of a heavy slug that took him in the chest. His knees gave way and he pitched to the ground in the alley.

Raven stepped into the doorway, levelling his pistol. He saw gun smoke drifting from the doorway of the barn at the rear, caught the furtive movement of a man just inside the building, and fired as the man lifted the pistol he was holding. The man dropped his gun and pitched forward on his face. Raven paused only to bend over Wilson. His lips pulled tight when he saw that the sheriff was dead.

Echoes of the shots were fading away across the town. Raven glanced around. The deputy who had been asleep on the chair in front of the office was peering around the front corner of the building. Raven snapped a shot in his direction and the man's head was hurriedly withdrawn. Raven departed at a run, moving quickly around the rear corner of the building. He lost himself in the clustered shanties and made his way back to the spot where he had left his horse.

He approached the animal carefully, expecting an ambush, but there was no one around. He tightened his cinch, stepped up into the saddle and rode out, watching his surroundings as he travelled. Moments later he was hammering along the open trail, heading back to Diamond Cross.

Raven's hard features were set grimly as he considered the situation. He had been used by everyone who had an interest in the crookedness, but the death of Sheriff Wilson changed matters a great deal, and Jackson was out of it now so there was no law to worry about. The wolves were coming out into the open, and Raven was certain that he could pick them off as and when they appeared. He urged the horse into its fastest gallop, wondering just what was happening out at the ranch. If Wilson had been telling the truth then an attack was being made on Diamond Cross right now.

A bullet crackled past his head from behind and he dived out of his saddle, dragging his rifle from its scabbard as he did so. More shots hammered and bullets struck the hard ground around his position. He rolled into a depression and worked the mechanism of his rifle, jacking a shell into the breech. A bullet jerked through the crown of his hat in passing and he reared up, saw a rider galloping towards him, and fired instantly. The rider pitched out of his saddle.

Raven paused, ready for more trouble, but saw nothing untoward. He got to his feet and looked around more intently. His horse was grazing several yards away. He fetched the animal, climbed into his saddle, and rode back to where his attacker lay. He was not surprised when he recognized the deputy who had been asleep in the chair in front of the law office in town. The man was dead.

For some moments Raven gazed down at the man. Then he shook his head and resumed his ride to Diamond Cross. He had covered several miles when he topped a rise in the trail and saw a tight group of six riders coming fast towards him. He reined about quickly and rode across the rise again until he was in cover.

He remained with his head showing above the rise, watching the oncoming riders while he drew his Winchester and cocked the weapon. His keen gaze soon picked out the figure of Clint Jackson leading the group, and his eyes narrowed when he saw that Jackson's companion was Homer Kirk, who had his leather bag suspended from his saddle horn. The four riders behind Jackson and Kirk looked like the possemen who had ridden into Diamond Cross earlier with the deputy. The group seemed to be in a great hurry.

Jackson reined in immediately when he saw Raven and the men with him did likewise. Raven watched them conferring, then Kirk turned his horse to his left and spurred the animal away. Raven lifted his rifle to his shoulder, sighted on the unfortunate horse, and fired instantly. Kirk's horse went down heavily, pushing its nose into the ground, its legs threshing. Kirk was thrown clear. He tried to get to his feet, staggered a couple of paces, then fell and lay inert. Raven listened to the echoes of the shot reverberating to the horizon.

Jackson spoke to his four men and

then came riding towards Raven while they held their position. The deputy put up his right hand as he came to the foot of the rise, where he halted and sat his mount, holding the animal on a tight rein.

'What is going on at Diamond Cross?' Raven demanded. 'Who turned you loose?'

'There's been a change of ownership out there.' Jackson grinned. 'Lorne Hallam has sold out to Ben Wisbee. It seems Hallam got in arrears with his mortgage and had to cut his losses. Wisbee foreclosed on him and has sold the spread to Monte Grand, who showed up with Wisbee and a dozen of the Big G outfit. They've taken over lock, stock and barrel. Looks like you are out of a job now, Raven. You better come back to town with me. I expect Grand has his outfit on the range now, looking for you. He reckons you're too dangerous to be left alive.'

'So that's the way the wind is blowing, huh?' Raven smiled. 'Monte

Grand is the kingpin, and he's come up with a plan to take over the ranch legally. Where is Beth now?'

'Sarah Jane took her to Wisbee's ranch. They loaded Lorne Hallam in a buckboard and took him along. Sheridan got himself shot trying to stop the deal but he ain't dead. The rest of the Diamond Cross crew pulled out. Grand paid them all off.'

'Where does Stig Ivey come into this?' Raven asked. 'He was in town but left before I got there.'

'Far as I know, Grand brought him in on his side soon as he heard about you coming up from Mexico to help Beth.'

Raven considered the situation, shaking his head while he searched his mind for his next move. Jackson was grinning. Raven was angered by the man's easy insolence.

'What are your plans now?' Raven demanded. 'You look like you're holding a winning hand.'

'I'm going back to town. Wilson will wanta know about the developments.'

'He won't, you know. He's dead.'

Jackson's face sobered at the news. Disbelief glimmered in his eyes. He swallowed, shaking his head.

'Who killed him?'

'Whoever he is, he's lying dead in the doorway of the barn back of the jail.'

Raven explained the incidents that had occurred in town.

'Tell me about the rustling you and Wilson were involved in,' he invited. 'Who were you working with?'

'I don't know a thing about any rustling.' Jackson shook his head emphatically. 'You're always trying to pile trouble on me.'

'Wilson told me what was going on before he was shot. The two of you were riding with Grand's outfit, cleaning out the ranches Grand figured to take over. It's no use denying it, Jackson. I got you dead to rights.'

'What's it to you now? You ain't got a job here any more. Beth brought you in to fight for Diamond Cross but she don't own it any more so you better quit while you can. You can't fight the set-up around here. Go back to Mexico. It'll be safer for you.'

'You'd quit if you were in my boots, huh? Well I ain't about to pull a stunt like that. Lift your gun and get to work, Jackson. You're high on my list for killing.'

'Now hold on.' Jackson shook his head. 'I ain't gonna draw against you.'

'That's too bad.' Raven laughed. 'You got five seconds to fill your hand.'

Jackson dropped his reins and lifted both hands shoulder high.

'I'm a legal deputy, and if you kill me you'll be hunted down by the law. You ain't the man to saddle yourself with that kind of a millstone.'

Raven lifted his rifle and fired the weapon without seeming to aim. Jackson's hat flew from his head. The deputy ducked, dived out of his saddle, and hit the ground hard. He rolled and came up shooting, his pistol clutched in his right hand and pointed at Raven. His slug crackled past Raven's head.

Raven fired instantly and a red splotch appeared in the centre of Jackson's forehead. The deputy dropped his gun and fell face down in the dust.

Pandemonium broke out among the four riders in the background. One of them hauled out his pistol while the other three spurred their horses and came galloping towards the rise, shooting sporadically. Raven returned fire. His first shot killed the man drawing the gun, and he turned his rifle on the other three as they began to shoot at him. The raucous sounds of gunfire bludgeoned the silence as the trio fell out of their saddles in rapid succession. Raven stopped shooting. He sat watching the grim scene until the last of the echoes had faded across the horizon.

Before riding on, Raven went to where Homer Kirk was lying. The man was dead, his neck broken. He picked up Kirk's bag and rode on to Diamond Cross.

10

When Raven reached Diamond Cross, shadows had closed in. He left his horse in cover beyond the rim of the valley and went forward on foot to look at the ranch headquarters. The sun had dropped below the horizon, leaving the sky aflame with orange and gold streaks of heavenly fire. The valley was shrouded, its western rim almost black, and the lights burning in the ranch house and the bunkhouse added to the density of the coming night. Two figures were moving around the yard, armed with rifles, and Raven nodded. The ranch had become an armed camp.

A furtive noise sounded close by, alerting Raven to danger. He palmed his gun as he gazed around. To his right, a man appeared out of the brush to look down at the ranch. Raven strained his eyes and recognized

Mason. He called the gunman's name. Mason dived back into the brush, and a moment later his voice sounded.

'Is that you, Raven?'

'Yeah. What's going on around here?'

Mason reappeared and came to where Raven was crouching. He dropped into cover.

'I'm glad to see you, Raven. I guessed you would show up, and I've been hanging around in the hope of spotting you before you rode into the valley. You must have seen Jackson on the trail or you wouldn't be here looking over the spread.'

'I met him. He's dead now, and so are the men who were with him.' Raven gave an account of what happened after he left Diamond Cross. 'When Jackson told me what went on here when Grand rode in with Wisbee, I reckoned the truth had come out at last.'

'It sure looks that way. Wisbee foreclosed on Hallam despite Beth saying there was plenty of dough in the ranch account. Wisbee denied that, so there must have been some trickery done at the bank. Grand told Wisbee to take Beth and Lorne Hallam to Wisbee's place, and, when they had gone, Grand fired the whole of the Diamond Cross crew. Sheridan pulled his gun in protest and was shot down. He's gone to town to see the doctor. The rest of the outfit left quietly, but they ain't going. They figure you won't quit, and they're prepared to fight if you want their help. They rode out to the south-west line camp, and will be waiting there for a couple of days.'

'Have you seen Stig Ivey around?'

'I don't know Ivey by sight, but a tough-looking man rode into the spread about an hour ago. I was up on the west rim at that time, keeping watch. That guy sure looked like he could be the whole Ivey gang by himself.'

'Describe him.'

'Big feller. Looked ugly as sin. He was dressed in black clothes. Even his hat was black, decorated with a silver hatband made of fancy-looking

Conchos. He looked like a dude, but I'd think twice before tangling with him. He had that look about him.'

'That sounds like Ivey.' Eagerness edged Raven's voice. 'Is he still on the spread?'

'No. He rode out with Grand half an hour ago. They headed for Big G.'

'Did any of Grand's men ride with Beth and her father?'

'A couple of gunnies. Wisbee and his daughter rode along as well.'

'Did it look like Beth and Hallam were prisoners?'

'Yeah. I reckon you got the rights of it. Maybe they're in a lot of trouble.'

Raven digested the information as he moved back from their vantage point.

'What are we gonna do?' Mason asked.

'Find out from Beth what the situation is. Take me to Wisbee's place.'

'Sure. It's about fifteen miles from here. I'll back your play, Raven. I don't like what's been going on around here. I heard a couple of Grand's gunnies

217

talking down there in the yard before we were all fired. Floyd Buxton was shot dead on the range. It looks like Grand's outfit is tidying up, taking care of anyone who might cause trouble. It makes me wonder what Grand has planned for Beth and the boss.'

'Let's get moving,' Raven said. 'If we're to put a knot in Grand's rope we need to get started. We'll have a good chance if we can put Beth in the clear.'

They went to their horses and rode out. Mason set a fast canter despite the uncertainty of the trail. Raven was occupied by his thoughts. He would never forgive himself if something bad happened to Beth. She might yet be safe, if the banker, Wisbee, was not in on the stealing with Grand. He cut through his thoughts, aware that his gun would solve all the problems once he had ensured Beth's safety.

It was late when Mason pointed out a light shining through the darkness.

'Wisbee's ranch, Bar W,' he observed.

'Is it a big spread?' Raven asked.

'No. Some small rancher didn't keep up his mortgage payments, and Wisbee took it over. He's keeping the place for Sarah Jane when she marries.'

They pushed on until Bar W rose up out of the range and took on the shape of a small ranch. Raven dismounted almost a hundred yards out from the back of the house and tied his horse to a bush. The night was not completely dark. Star-shine added a silvery deceptiveness to the shadows, and a thin sliver of the moon was showing away to the east.

'Maybe you'll stay here, Mason,' he said. 'It's my job to handle trouble, and I work better alone.'

'Like hell! I draw gun wages, and now I better start earning them.'

Raven nodded and walked towards the dark pile of the house. There was no light in any of the rear windows. He eased along the side of the house until he reached the front corner. Light was issuing from the two big front windows overlooking the porch, throwing long

219

shafts of yellow glare into the yard. A man armed with a rifle was standing on the porch. Raven palmed his gun. A board creaked when he stepped on to the porch, and the guard swung quickly to face him.

'Keep your muzzle pointing at the sky,' Raven said harshly.

The guard froze. Mason stepped around Raven and disarmed the man.

'Who's in the house?' Raven demanded.

'The Wisbees are here. They got company over from Diamond Cross.'

'Who do you ride for, Wisbee or Monte Grand?'

'Wisbee, of course. There are a couple of Grand's men in the house.'

'Watch him, Mason, while I check out the house,' Raven said.

He peered through one of the big front windows into a large room and saw Sarah Jane Wisbee seated at a big table. A man in his fifties, well dressed in a blue store suit, was sitting at a big desk situated in a corner, and a younger man was lounging in a big easy chair beside a smaller table.

'Take a look, Mason, and put names to the two men,' Raven said. 'I'll watch the prisoner.'

He covered the guard while Mason approached the window.

'The older man is Wisbee,' Mason reported. 'The other one is Cal Boyd, one of Monte Grand's top guns. There should be another of Grand's men around.'

'Sure. Stay out here until I've handled Boyd, then bring this guy in.' Raven moved to the big front door.

He tried the door. It opened noiselessly to his touch and he entered the house, cocking his gun as he walked into the room. Cal Boyd looked up, and became very still when he saw Raven's menacing figure. Then he reached instinctively for his guns, thought better of it, and moved his hands away from his waist. He sat gazing fixedly at Raven.

'You got sense,' Raven said. 'Get up,

unbuckle your gun belts, drop them, and move away.' He waited until the man had complied. 'Now get down on the floor and put your arms above your head. You so much as blink and I'll kill you.'

Boyd obeyed without hesitation. Raven looked at Wisbee. The banker had moved his right hand inside his jacket to his left armpit. He stopped the movement when he saw Raven watching him.

'If it's a gun you've got there then take it out and toss it on the floor. Get smart and you'll get killed.' Raven waited until the banker had complied and, when a short-barrelled pistol thudded on the floor, he turned his attention to Sarah Jane, who had remained motionless.

'Where are Beth and her father?' he asked.

'In one of the bedrooms,' she replied. 'A gunman is guarding them.'

Raven nodded and backed to the front door. He motioned for Mason to enter, and the gunman ushered in their prisoner.

'So far, so good,' Mason observed looking around the room.

'Watch these people,' Raven told him.

He went to the desk and studied the banker's taut face for some moments. Wisbee was in his middle fifties, short and fleshy, with a wrinkled face and narrowed brown eyes. He was pale-complexioned, as if he had spent more time out of the sun than in it. He met Raven's gaze stolidly, his eyes narrowed, calculating.

'Tell me about the steal involving Diamond Cross,' Raven said. 'You're working with Monte Grand to take the ranch away from the Hallams, huh?'

'I don't know anything about that.' Wisbee moved uneasily in his seat. 'Lorne Hallam got behind with his mortgage repayments and I had to foreclose. Monte Grand offered to buy the spread, and I had no option but to accept his offer.'

'That sounds reasonable, and I'd accept it but for one thing.' Raven smiled. 'Why are the Hallams here now, under guard?'

Wisbee shrugged and remained silent. Raven regarded him for a moment before asking:

'Are you involved in the rustling?'

'What do you take me for?'

'I'm merely asking. I learned that the sheriff and his deputy were bossing the rustling, aided by Monte Grand's outfit, and as you're in on stealing the ranch then you're probably involved in the rest of this crooked business.'

Wisbee grimaced. 'I don't know anything about Monte's business interests.'

'Wilson and Jackson are dead. I'll kill anyone working against Beth. You're holding Beth prisoner, and that brings me in against you.'

'They're not prisoners.' Wisbee shook his head emphatically. His pale complexion had turned ashen, and he moistened his dry lips. 'They're free to leave any time. Lorne isn't up to travelling far, and I offered to let them stay here until they can make arrangements to leave the county.'

'Why do I disbelieve you?' Raven motioned with his gun. 'Let's go up and talk to them, huh? On your feet. You lead the way.'

Wisbee got up and crossed the room to the stairs towards the rear. Raven followed closely, gun covering the banker's spine. They ascended the stairs, and Raven saw a man seated on a chair outside a bedroom. The man got to his feet when he saw Wisbee, and frowned at Raven. He began to lower his hand to his hip. Raven showed his drawn gun and the man froze.

'Don't do anything stupid,' Raven said. He moved around Wisbee and snaked a weapon out of the man's holster. 'Open the door and go into the room.'

The man produced a key, unlocked the door, and led the way into the room. Raven pushed Wisbee forward and followed closely. Lorne Hallam was lying on the big double bed in the room, and Beth was seated on a straight-back chair. It was the first time Raven had seen Lorne Hallam, who was still suffering from the effects of the bullet that had struck him down. His face was pale, his eyes closed, and he did not stir when Beth sprang up with a cry of relief. She ran across the room to Raven, exclaiming excitedly.

'I just knew you'd show up!' she declared, casting a venomous glance at Wisbee. 'What a skunk he turned out to be! You'll never guess what he's trying to pull. And Monte Grand is running it. I've said all along that he was involved.'

'I've heard some of it,' Raven said, 'and you can tell me the rest later. I know enough to start cleaning up, but first I need to get you and your pa to a place of safety.'

'We'll go back to Diamond Cross.' Beth spoke without hesitation. She turned on the motionless Wisbee. 'What have you been up to?' she demanded. 'How could you foreclose on us? Our account has always been in the black, and we've never missed a mortgage payment. If our account is empty then you have stolen the money.'

'Wisbee will recheck your accounts when he can get around to it, and he'll be more careful, with me looking over his shoulder.' Raven met Wisbee's gaze, and the banker shrugged. 'I'll be seeing Monte Grand first chance I get, and when I've settled him he won't be interested in any kind of business. You've got time to think over your dealings, Wisbee, and you better straighten out Diamond Cross before I get to you again.'

'He'll certainly do that,' Beth said. 'If he won't, I'll take a gun to him.'

Wisbee opened his mouth to reply, but a shot hammered somewhere downstairs, blanking out his voice. Raven reacted instinctively. He gave Beth the weapon he had taken from the guard.

'Stay up here with your father, lock the door on the inside, and shoot

227

anyone who tries to get in at you,' he ordered. 'You two, down the stairs ahead of me.'

Beth took the gun, a tight smile on her lips. Raven grinned at her and followed Wisbee and the guard out to the stairs. They descended to find Mason standing by the front door, which he had opened a couple of inches, his gun in his hand. Raven saw that Colby and the guard were now bound hand and foot. Sarah Jane was still motionless at the table, her head in her hands.

'What was that shot?' Raven demanded.

'Someone opened the door and I fired to discourage him,' Mason replied. 'I heard a bunch of riders coming into the yard just before that.'

'Bind Wisbee and the guard,' Raven said. 'I'll handle whatever comes up.'

Mason grinned as he obeyed. Raven stood by the door, gun in hand. He could see nothing beyond the porch. The riders had halted well out of range.

Then someone called stridently, and Raven recognized Monte Grand's voice.

'Wisbee, where the hell are you? Why aren't my two men on guard?'

'It ain't going as you planned it, Grand,' Raven replied tauntingly. 'I've taken over here, and your crooked scheme has folded.'

'Spread out men and go to it,' Grand yelled instantly.

A gun boomed and flashed in the darkness of the yard, and the next instant a fusillade of shots thudded into the front wall of the ranch house.

Raven closed and bolted the door. He looked around the big room. Mason was finishing his job of trussing Wisbee and the guard. Sarah Jane still sat motionless at the table, and did not flinch when a bullet smashed one of the front windows, zipped across the room and smacked into the rear wall.

'Take Sarah Jane upstairs and leave her with Beth,' Raven said.

Mason nodded and grasped the girl's arm. She went with him willingly.

Raven heaved a sigh as he looked around the big room. There were too many windows in it for an easy defence. He saw a rifle hanging on two pegs below the big painting on the chimney breast and crossed to it, holstering his pistol. The rifle was a fifteen-shot repeater, fully loaded, and he cocked it, smiling. Mason returned, and Raven checked the bonds on their four prisoners.

'OK, blow out the lamp,' Raven said, and the room was plunged into near darkness.

Raven's eyes gradually became accustomed to the shadows. He stayed back from the front windows, covering them all, and warned Mason to watch those on the right. At least eight guns were shooting at the house, racketing the night with blaring sound. Glass was shattered and bullets crackled through the close darkness. Raven dropped to one knee, waiting for the initial storm to pass. There were two big front windows in the room, and smaller ones in the side walls. His narrowed gaze flitted from one window to another as he awaited the inevitable assault.

A hand tried the front door. Raven fired through the thick planks and a body fell heavily to the porch. The volume of shooting dwindled and died away.

'Come out and I'll let you ride away,' Grand called. 'It ain't your fight.'

'No dice.' Raven smiled. 'I'm in this until you're down in the dust, Grand. What are you waiting for? I'm ready for you. Cut the cackle and let's get to it.'

The shooting was renewed furiously and the big room was blasted by hammering slugs. A shapeless figure appeared at a side window and crashed out the remaining glass with a rifle butt. Raven snapped a shot and the figure disappeared as if wiped away by a giant hand. Raven's eyes glinted. His lips pulled back in a grimace that was half smile, half snarl. He held the rifle in his shoulder, the butt cuddled against his jaw.

Boots thudded on the porch. Then a heavy object crashed against the stout door, shaking it, splintering one of its thick planks. Raven fired rapidly, sending six shots through the door as it was smashed from its hinges. The doorway became blocked by a rush of men striving to get in despite the flailing bullets that riddled them. Smoke drifted as guns hammered. Raven worked the mechanism of the rifle, tossing lead into the centre of the rush. Shadowy figures stumbled and fell, and the heavy detonations of the shooting were edged with hoarse shouts and anguished cries, the close darkness split by criss-crossing streaks of muzzle flame.

The ghastly tableau was maintained for interminable moments. Raven fired without aiming, shooting into the mass. He could hear Mason's gun at work in the background, firing at shadows appearing at the windows. Then the action cut off and an uneasy silence fell as gun echoes faded. Raven heard the hammer of the rifle click and knew the weapon was empty. He discarded it and drew his Colt, then waited for the next rush.

'We've got 'em beat, Raven.' Mason's voice came from the right. 'How many men can Grand have out there?'

'It doesn't matter how many.' Raven wrinkled his nose against gun smoke.

'Yeah. They've got to come in and settle us before they can win,' Mason observed 'and I don't see them handling that. We've got 'em by the tail with a downward pull.'

A heavy hammering sounded somewhere at the back of the house.

'I'll take care of it,' Mason said.

Raven heard Mason's boots pounding the floor, and moments later the gun man was firing through the back door. The shooting died away and echoes fled into the night. Silence came and tension filtered through the uneasy atmosphere.

'Damn you, Raven! You got no chance here. Before I left Diamond

Cross I sent a man to my ranch for the rest of my crew, and they'll be turning up soon.'

Raven did not bother to reply. He reloaded his pistol and stood waiting easily, watching the windows. Mason returned from the back door.

'It's quiet out back now,' he reported. 'I reckon we've nailed all the men Grand brought with him.'

'I'll go out and look around while you remain alert in here,' Raven said.

'Sure thing. Sing out when you wanta come back in.'

Raven's boots crunched on broken glass as he walked to the shattered door. Five men were lying in a heap in the doorway, and one was groaning. Raven bent and removed weapons. He stuck an extra pistol in his waistband and pulled the wounded man out of the doorway. The thick smell of gun smoke filled his nostrils as he peered out at the silent porch, studying the shadows around the front of the house. The night was still. He waited patiently for movement but nothing disturbed the silence, and he began to accept that Monte Grand had pulled out with his surviving men.

Gun in his hand, Raven went through the doorway and eased along the porch, flattening against the front wall. He moved slowly to his right until he was standing at the corner of the house, then eased down to the boards of the porch until he was lying on his belly. He stuck his head around the corner, gun ready in his deadly hand, saw nothing to cause alarm, and eased off the porch to flatten his big figure against the wall of the house. He dropped to the ground and crawled out from the wall until he was twenty yards clear of the building, then began to make a circuit, moving around to the left, looking for Grand or his men.

He was directly in front of the shattered front door when a horse stamped somewhere out beyond the gate. He turned to investigate, crawling slowly, and suddenly saw a group of

235

riders huddled together outside the gate. He caught a glimpse of starlight glinting on drawn weapons. There were nine men, and he assumed them to be Grand's outfit. He lay watching, his gun covering them.

'Well there ain't no shooting now,' someone said in a harsh voice. 'No lights and no sound. What do you make of it, Buck?'

'I don't like it,' a low voice replied. 'Tudman said he saw Wisbee bringing Beth and the boss out of Diamond Cross, and they headed this way under guard. We saw Monte Grand riding in the direction of his spread a few minutes ago. So what's going on?'

Raven grinned as he recognized Buck Fuller's voice.

'I'll tell you what's going on,' he called, and the sound of his voice caused momentary confusion among the riders. They spread out, and Raven heard the sound of guns being cocked. 'This is Raven,' he continued. 'If you're the Diamond Cross crew then sing out loud and clear.'

'Raven? Heck, yes, we're Diamond Cross. I'm Buck Fuller.'

Raven got to his feet. 'You're just in time for the showdown,' he said. 'Monte Grand has gone back to his ranch for the rest of his crew. There's gonna be a battle when the sun comes up. I've got Wisbee prisoner in the house, and Beth and her pa are holding out in a bedroom. Mason is with me, and we could sure do with some help.'

'That's what we're here for.' Fuller dismounted. 'When Wisbee paid us off I told Mason we'd be at the line shack waiting for a call from you. I knew something was wrong when we didn't get any word so we came on here. We heard shooting, but it was all over by the time we arrived. We needed to know what was going on before we pitched in.'

'Let's go into the house and I'll lay it out for you,' Raven responded.

Mason was overjoyed when he saw the newcomers. Raven told Fuller to put out guards and prepare for an attack.

'I'll take Mason with me and we'll scout towards Diamond Cross,' Raven said. 'If I kill Monte Grand, the trouble will die with him. Go and let Beth know you're here, Fuller, and hold this place until I get back.'

The foreman nodded agreement, his face grim. Raven turned to Mason.

'We'll get our horses and make tracks,' he said. 'I want to settle this business before breakfast.'

They departed, and when they were mounted, Mason led the way unerringly through the night towards Diamond Cross. Raven sat slumped in his saddle, tired but mentally alert and ready for action. They rode steadily. Raven wanted to be able to see his targets when shooting was resumed, and planned to reach Diamond Cross as the sun came up.

Dawn was breaking when they reined up on a rise and saw the Hallam ranch headquarters huddled before them. They dismounted and loosened cinches. The horses began to graze while they lay in cover awaiting sunlight.

Full daylight arrived with the first rays of the sun probing across the eastern horizon. Raven stood up and stretched. He attended to his horse and swung into the saddle. Mason was gazing down at the ranch.

'Hey, take a look,' he called.

Raven moved forward and saw four riders crossing the yard to the gate. The foremost was Monte Grand.

'Looks like we're in luck,' Raven said. 'If we move to the right we'll be ready for them if they turn in this direction. Can you recognize any of the men with Grand? I thought he left Wisbee's place to fetch the rest of his outfit. If three is all he can find then he won't get his job done, not by a long rope.'

'They're strangers,' Mason said after studying the riders. 'They're coming this way. Do we ambush them?'

'We'll stay in cover and get the drop on them,' Raven decided. 'I'll move out

239

to the right so they'll come between us. If they want to fight, we'll feed 'em hot lead.'

Mason moved into cover while Raven edged out to the right and positioned himself to get the riders at a slight angle. Grand was riding slightly ahead of his men, and they came at a fast clip along the faint trail that led to the Wisbee ranch. Raven drew his pistol and checked it. He returned the weapon to his holster and kept his hand close to his hip. As the riders drew nearer, Raven looked over the three men following Grand, and shock hit him when he recognized the harsh features of Stig Ivey. The outlaw was riding a big black stallion. He was wearing twin pistols on crossed cartridge belts, and his right hand was down on his thigh, ready to slip into action at the first sign of trouble.

Raven gazed at the man he had trailed for months. The outlaw had dropped out of circulation then, but he was here now, riding brazenly along the open trail. Raven could not define his innermost feelings. He had prayed for this day to arrive, and his pulses raced with anticipation as he steeled himself to confront the man who had been responsible for the deaths of his mother and brother.

Monte Grand was only yards from the spot where Raven was waiting when Mason rode out of cover. The gunman was holding his pistol in his hand, ready to do battle. Grand checked his horse at Mason's movement, and called a warning to his three companions. Raven showed himself then, kneeing his horse forward.

Grand reached for his holstered gun in a fast draw, his attention on Mason. The Diamond Cross gunman started triggering his Colt, and Monte Grand jerked back in his saddle as a bullet took him in the chest. Raven was in the open now, and pulled his horse in, reins in his left hand. Grand was falling out of his saddle. Raven had eyes only for Ivey and the two men with him.

Ivey was reaching for his guns, intent upon Mason, when Raven called.

'Hold it, Ivey. I'm Raven. I've been looking for you a long time.'

The trio of outlaws froze, turning their heads to look at Raven. Mason waited, gun uplifted. Ivey stared at Raven, his hands gripping the butts of his guns, his knees controlling his horse. Grand was lying forward over the neck of his horse, clutching at the animal's mane. He was trying to bring his pistol to bear on Mason, but the weapon seemed to be too heavy for him and he dropped it before following it into the dust.

Ivey grinned and started his draw. His pistols jerked from their holsters. Raven followed the outlaw's play. His gun swept up and levelled, his thumb cocking the weapon before the muzzle was lined up on Ivey's figure. The outlaw was slower by a split second. His finger was tightening on his trigger as Raven's shot hammered into his chest and blasted out his life.

Mason drove lead at the two outlaws in the background. One dropped instantly, and Raven fired again, killing the second man while Stig Ivey was still falling out of his saddle.

Raven sat motionless, gripping his gun, his gaze on the crumpled figure of the dead gang boss. He had closed the account. Echoes of the shooting were growling around the horizon when he straightened and holstered his deadly gun. He looked at Mason, who was watching him intently.

'It looks like we've shot our way out of trouble,' he said. 'Let's get back to Wisbee's place and play the last hand in this crooked game. I reckon I can be on my way back to Mexico tomorrow.'

They turned their horses and rode back the way they had come. Raven gazed ahead, his thoughts idle, keenly aware now that he did not want to return to Mexico. He straightened his shoulders. With a little luck, he thought, Beth Hallam might offer him a permanent job, nursing cows or mending fences. He certainly did not want to use his guns again.

THE END

We do hope that you have enjoyed reading this large print book.

Did you know that all of our titles are available for purchase?

We publish a wide range of high quality large print books including:
**Romances, Mysteries, Classics
General Fiction
Non Fiction and Westerns**

Special interest titles available in large print are:
**The Little Oxford Dictionary
Music Book, Song Book
Hymn Book, Service Book**

Also available from us courtesy of Oxford University Press:
**Young Readers' Dictionary
(large print edition)
Young Readers' Thesaurus
(large print edition)**

For further information or a free brochure, please contact us at:
**Ulverscroft Large Print Books Ltd.,
The Green, Bradgate Road, Anstey,
Leicester, LE7 7FU, England.
Tel:** (00 44) **0116 236 4325**
Fax: (00 44) **0116 234 0205**

AMBUSH IN DUST CREEK

Scott Connor

When Marshal Lincoln Hawk rode into the lawless town of Dust Creek his mission was to clean out its trigger-happy outlaws. Lincoln's deadly Peacemaker did just that, but some of the outlaws escaped. Years later, when Lincoln rides into Dust Creek again, the town seems to have been abandoned. But it hasn't. Mason Black and his outlaw band are waiting for him. From behind every broken window, Mason's guns are aimed at his head. To see another dawn, Lincoln must face a desperate battle for survival . . .

SILVER GULCH FEUD

Scott Connor

Yick Lee and Carter Lyle realize that they've picked the wrong day to start working for Lorne Wayne. For two years Lorne has feuded with Alistair Marriott over the ownership of the Silver Gulch mine. But now the mine's giant protection man, Abe Mountain, is hell-bent on ripping apart that feud by blasting into oblivion anyone who stands in his way. Lee and Carter battle to uncover buried truths about the mine. But can they succeed and Abe's guns be silenced?

RETURN OF THE VALKO KID

Michael D. George

Marshal Clem Everett is summoned to Austin by Governor Hyram Sloane to track down a gang of outlaws led by Black Bill Bodie. His mission is to recover a document Bodie has stolen. Bodie is the fastest draw alive and only the outlaw Valko Kid has any chance of beating Black Bill. Sloane agrees to pardon Valko if the pair can retrieve the document. Clem Everett and the Valko Kid set off after Bodie to face untold carnage in their quest.

BUSHWHACKER

Bill Morrison

When Hal Coburn returned from the Civil War, he hoped to resume his former peaceful life. Instead he found a homecoming of hostility and a dark memory that haunted the minds of all who looked at him. Justice and revenge are often hard to separate and where there is no help from the law only the gun can even the score. Bushwhacking seems a low way of searching for justice, the result can be as savage as war itself, as Hal was to discover.